STARPACKER

Hunter checked his colt over for one last time. He stepped outside, into a deserted street save for the man who'd called him out, who stood twenty yards away. This was it: the moment when you drew your gun for more than just to shatter empty bottles or blast the tips off Apache plumes — to kill.

*Books by David Whitehead
in the Linford Western Library:*

HELLER

DAVID WHITEHEAD

STARPACKER

Complete and Unabridged

LINFORD
Leicester

First published in Great Britain in 1990 by
Robert Hale Limited
London

First Linford Edition
published July 1992
by arrangement with
Robert Hale Limited
London

British Library CIP Data

Whitehead, David *1958* –
Starpacker.—Large print ed.—
Linford western library
I. Title II. Series
823.914 [F]

ISBN 0–7089–7184–9

Published by
F. A. Thorpe (Publishing) Ltd.
Anstey, Leicestershire
Set by Words & Graphics Ltd.
Anstey, Leicestershire
Printed and bound in Great Britain by
T. J. Press (Padstow) Ltd., Padstow, Cornwall

For Rusty and Gus

1

THE old woman sitting outside the ramshackle cabin was plucking feathers from a chicken she'd just strangled when she first spied the rider coming out of the heat-haze to the north.

As she watched him ride nearer, her dull, almost black eyes narrowed slightly against the early-morning glare. Visitors were rare in these parts. Always had been. But not once did her short, rough fingers pause in their work. She just kept plucking away as if nothing else mattered, dropping the feathers into a soft pile between her thick, vein-threaded legs.

She must have been seventy or so, dressed in a flowery old smock that no longer accommodated all her bulges. Her hair was grey and lifeless, a sharp contrast to the deep tan of her wrinkled and seamed old face.

The small, run-down homestead around her was in desperate need of repair. There was a broken-walled well with a bucket tied to a length of worn hemp, a dilapidated barn, a wheel-less wagon up on blocks. The porch upon which she sat seemed to droop right into the dust. Only sparse patches of brush, a few distorted cacti and a scattering of skeletal trees provided any relief from the otherwise deadening view on all sides.

The rider came closer, slowing his strawberry roan to a walk, then reining back altogether once he reached the front yard.

He was a tall, rangy man dressed in a plain calico work-shirt, hard-wearing levis, high-heeled boots and a dusty, dun-coloured stetson, and his long, sunburned face — host to a straight, sharp nose, sad mouth and square jaw — was unremarkable save for the strange, restless quality of his grey eyes.

Man and horse were yellowed with alkali from the flats they'd just crossed. The man was in his late twenties; his eyes, however, looked much older.

On the surface he could have been just another drifter. *Could* have been. But the way he held his horse's reins in his left hand, keeping the right close to the wooden grips of his Frontier Colt, suggested that he was much more.

He sat his saddle politely, not wanting to dismount until invited. He smiled gently at the old woman, but she did not smile back. From somewhere behind the cabin he heard a couple of chickens squabbling in the dust and the mournful call of a malnourished cow.

"Good mornin', ma'am," he said at last.

By way of reply she said, "Stranger."

When it was obvious that she wasn't going to say any more, he asked, "Could you spare some water for me and my horse, ma'am?"

"He'p y'self," she replied.

He climbed down from the saddle

3

and led his mount across to the well, where he lowered the old bucket and waited quietly for it to fill.

The air was still and warm, drying the sweat to salt on his skin. He could feel the itchy dampness between his shoulder-blades and beneath his arms, but when the old woman's black eyes fell on him, he forgot the heat and very nearly shivered.

He wound the bucket back up, took his canteen and filled it, capped it and tied it back around his pommel. He took a mouthful of water for himself, then filled his stetson and held it to the roan's muzzle, allowing the animal to drink just enough and no more.

"Warm day," he said.

"Like most days," the old woman allowed.

He spilled the excess water from his hat and put it back on, enjoying the cool, damp band it pressed across his forehead. Then he took up the horse's reins and reached into his shirt pocket, bringing out a stack of silver dollars, ten in all. He put them on the porch next to the woman and mounted up.

"For your kindness,' ma'am," he said, clucking the horse. "Come on, boy."

But the old woman's cracked voice stopped him. "Water ain't that 'spensive," she muttered. "Not even out here."

She picked up the stack of coins, studying them through narrow eyes, and her lips compressed into a grim line. Suddenly the day seemed to grow more stifling, and the young man on the strawberry roan wanted desperately just to ride away.

But then the woman returned her black eyes to his face, and he felt compelled to offer her some kind of explanation.

"It ain't much," he said awkwardly. "But it might help. I mean . . . I understand you lost your man a while back."

Something moved within her eyes then; not tears or gratitude or the faint stirring of painful memories, but recognition. And then hatred.

"You're Hunter," she said, making his name sound more like a curse. She began to tremble with rage, the half-plucked chicken still gripped in her rough hands but now forgotten.

Reluctantly he nodded. "Yes'm. I'm Hunter. But listen, you got to try and understan — "

"I understand!" she spat. "I understand that you're a thievin', no-good murderer!" Spittle flew in the air as she began to curse him.

Hunter's fingers whitened around the reins. It was useless to try and make her listen, to convince her that —

But what the hell? He should've known better than to ride in here with ten silver dollars in his pocket and hope that he could make up for what she thought he had done six long years before.

Angry with himself, he turned the horse to go, but just then a young girl appeared in the doorway of the old house. She was in her mid-twenties, with a smooth, clear face, large brown eyes, an expressive mouth and a small, straight nose. Fair hair framed her face, hair the colour of corn, and her body, although hidden beneath a dark skirt and blouse, was curvy and mature.

"Ma! What's goin' on out here?"

Without looking around, the old woman said hoarsely, "It's him, Bonnie. The one as killed your pa, God rest him."

The girl's face went slack at the revelation, and Hunter saw surprise flare in her eyes. Before she too could confront him, he clucked the roan into a canter, back out onto the open desert.

"The Lord damn you, murderer!" the old woman yelled, throwing the silver dollars so that they fell like alien rain against his back.

"Ma," the young girl said worriedly, her arms going out to comfort her trembling mother. "Come on, ma." As she hugged the older woman, she watched Hunter ride back into the shimmering heat-haze. "Was that *really* him?" she asked quietly.

Tears filled the old woman's eyes as she nodded. Then, through clenched, yellowed teeth, she hissed. "You can't buy my man's life with no amount o' silver dollars, mister, an' you should'a known better'n to even try!"

Two days and thirty miles later, the memory of that brief but unpleasant encounter still stung Hunter. He told himself that he was a fool, that he should never have come back, and yet . . . and yet he knew it would have been impossible for him *not* to have come back.

A flock of wild geese crossed the cloudless sky, but he paid them no heed. With his mind elsewhere, he allowed the roan to pick its own way across the shallow stream they'd been following for almost two hours, his young, sun-bronzed face moody and troubled.

Around him starflowers, chinaberries, loco and milkweed waved gently in a warm breeze. Flies buzzed through the muggy air and lizards and bullfrogs darted back and forth in the long grass fringing the trail. Every so often disturbed fish popped the surface of the sluggish stream.

The roan climbed up onto the far bank, through a stubble of blue grama. Man and horse crested a ridge, and the animal came to a halt at Hunter's light tug on the reins.

The man's restless grey eyes narrowed as he looked down at the town spread out in the rock-strewn basin below him, his spirits lifting slightly. Carver, Arizona Territory. He was here at last.

This, he told himself soberly, was either the beginning — or the end.

From this distance, the buildings formed a patchwork of stone; brick and timber. He spied clapboard houses and false-fronted saloons, a bank and a barber-shop, a dry-goods store and a drapery, a church or two, a freight company and a Western Union office.

Hunter sighed heavily, Carver. Population just under a thousand. He must've seen a hundred towns just like it in his twenty-seven years. But somehow this one was different. This town held the key to his destiny. He *knew* it.

"Come on, boy," he told the horse softly. "We got some scores to settle."

He clucked the roan back into motion.

Several people were going about their business on Front Street as he rode into town, although he knew that this wasn't the busiest time of day.

Men in suits hurried along the boardwalks. Women in shawls and large hats exchanged pleasantries on street corners. Hunter glanced left, saw neat little houses set back from the main stem, then right, to see the offices of the bi-weekly Carver *Star*, and smiled briefly at the sound of kids yelling fit to bust down at the local schoolhouse.

Keeping the roan to a walk, he passed the marshal's office, an adobe building with two small, barred windows and a thick wooden door, considered going straight in, then changed his mind. There was plenty of time for that after a beer. And he'd been on the trail for so long that he reckoned he'd earned a drink.

He angled across Front towards a two-storey drinking-parlour that called itself the Oriental Sunset, where he dismounted and hitched the roan to the rack outside.

His boots sounded loud against the hollow boards as he pushed through the batwings. It took a couple of seconds for his eyes to adjust to the gloom.

The room was long, with kerosene lanterns hanging from the low ceiling. He skirted a mess of tables and chairs to get to the bar, behind which stood a white-shirted dispenser of cheer and four shelves stocked with different brands of liquor.

Hunter bellied up between four big

men in buckskins at one end of the counter and a couple of townsmen nursing drinks at the other, their dusty boots hooked on the rail. In one corner, an old-timer sat whittling away at a piece of wood.

The bartender came forward to place his hairy hands on the counter. Beside Hunter, the four big men fairly exploded with laughter at some hastily-muttered joke. "Good morning, friend. Name yer pizzen."

"Beer."

"That'll be five cents."

Hunter fished out a couple of coins, laid them on the bartop and accepted a foaming mug. As he took his first sip, one of the buckskin-clad drinkers turned to face him.

"Hope you left yore herd outside'a town, cowboy," he growled. "I do purely hate the smell of cow-dung."

Hunter threw a casual glance into the mirror behind the bar, sizing up the quartet. They were all cut from the same cloth — big, heavy men whose faces were coppered and creased. All favoured woollen shirts along with their buckskins, the clothes stained with grease and sweat, torn and patched-up many times. One of them wore a flowing moustache, the other three long, shaggy beards.

The one who had spoken had a big black beard that covered most of his wide, high-cheekboned face. His eyes were black, too, just like the old woman's, and at some time or other someone had broken his nose, because now it was flat, the nostrils constantly flared. He could have been forty or fifty; it was difficult to tell.

"Don't worry," Hunter replied, trying to sound amiable. "I left the herd all the way back in Texas."

The big man frowned. "You sure?" he asked sceptically.

Hunter took another pull at the beer. "About as sure as I can get," he said evenly.

"Then how come I smell cow-dung now?"

Hunter didn't want trouble, but he set his schooner down fast and spun to face the other man. He could feel his temper slipping but fought hard to keep it in check.

"I mean, when was the last time you changed yore under-drawers, buddy?" the big man went on, clearly trying to goad him.

In the background, his red-faced, equally-inebriated cronies watched with anticipation lighting their bloodshot eyes.

Slowly Hunter's hands began to fold into fists. He didn't know why the big man had chosen to pick on him. Maybe because he was a stranger, new to town. But if he wanted trouble so badly, then Hunter was willing to oblige.

But no . . . no . . . *Calm down*. with a supreme effort he managed to cool off once again. He'd been a long time getting to this moment. He couldn't afford to spoil his chances now.

Sucking in a deep breath, he willed

14

his fists to relax and said, "You're drunk, big feller. Why don't you just go on home and sleep it off?"

The big man glared down at him, a wide, lopsided grin slowly spreading across his ugly, crumpled face. "Why don't you make me?" he countered.

The men at the other end of the counter were watching Hunter closely now. They all were. It was very quiet inside the Oriental Sunset.

"Aw, come in Ike," the bartender said, reaching across to punch the big man on the shoulder. "You know I don't like no grief in this place."

The big man kept his eyes on Hunter for another long beat, then returned his gaze to the bartender. "Awright, Casey. I don't figure this guy's got any backbone worth breakin' anyhow."

Hunter's jaw muscles worked hard. His breathing came fast, shallow. He wanted to knock that stupid smile right off the big man's face but kept telling himself that it wasn't worth it, that there was more at stake, too much

15

to risk on one oven-hot moment of anger. Still, he'd been passive for too long. The urge to hit back now was almost beyond control.

"Gimme another bottle o' that jig-juice," Ike — the big man — demanded, holding out one work-roughened paw.

The bartender quickly did as he was told, while one of the big man's friends threw some change down on the bar.

Ike closed his fist round the bottle, almost enveloping it whole; then, with another dark-eyed glare at Hunter, he turned and said, "Come on, fellers, let's go drink where the air's a mite cleaner."

The four of them headed for the batwings, muttering and sniggering, finally bursting into more sarcastic laughter just before they stepped out onto the street and disappeared from sight.

Hunter, watching them go, suddenly sensed the bartender leaning close to him across the counter. "They didn't mean no harm, friend," he muttered softly. "They're just a little joyful is all."

Hunter nodded. "I guess."

"Another?" the bartender asked, indicating the schooner between them. "On the house?"

"Sure. Why not?"

"I'm Casey, by the way. Joshua T. Casey."

"Tom Hunter. Pleased to know you."

Before the bartender went to work on filling a fresh mug, they shook.

"Still," said Hunter, glancing back at the batwings, "it's a little early in the day for a man to be that 'joyful' isn't it?"

Casey chuckled. "It's never too early for Ike Daggett and his crew, mister. They work down at the freight company. Boss's outta town on business, so . . . well, you know what, they say."

"While the cat's away . . . "

"You got it," Casey replied. He wiped a wet circle off the bartop. "Just rode in?"

"Yep."

"Lookin' for work or just passin' through?"

"Hoping for work."

"Well, you could do worse than rest up a while in Carver," the bartender said with a smile. "This little town's goin' places, Hunter. Believe me."

They swapped small-talk for a while as Hunter allowed the second beer to settle more comfortably inside his stomach. Now that Daggett and his cronies had gone, the atmosphere became altogether more sociable. But there was work to be done, much work and Hunter couldn't wait to start.

Back on the street, he took up the reins and walked his roan across to the marshal's office and stepped up onto the boardwalk. He took a deep breath and rapped sharply on the thick wooden door. Then he twisted the handle and went inside.

There was a kid of about eighteen summers sitting behind the desk. He had straight fair hair and pale-blue

18

eyes, and he looked as if he fitted in with his surroundings about as well as a mutton-puncher on a cattle-drive. He sat up, trying to assume an air of importance, and said, "Help you, stranger?"

Hunter released his breath. His mouth felt dry despite the beer he'd just consumed. But there was no going back now; he was committed.

"I've come about the job," he said. "As town marshal."

It had been a valuable piece of information he'd picked up about a month before; that Carver was looking for a new lawman.

He'd hardly been able to believe his luck. If he could just swing it so that he got the job, he'd have the perfect reason to hang around town and make enquiries about the man he was after; and there'd be quite a few of those, he was sure, before he located his quarry.

"I wired your mayor about a fortnight

ago," Hunter went on when the younker made no immediate response. "He should be expecting me."

At last the boy stood up and offered one thin hand. He was dressed in a check shirt and crisp new canvas pants. When he smiled he looked a little more at ease. As Hunter shook with him, the boy said, "I'm Zeb Coulson. Been lookin' after the office since Marshal Dabney left. Applied for the job myself, but they wouldn't let me have it. Said I was too young and a mite inexperienced."

Hunter introduced himself, running his eyes around the office. It was like a lot of other pokeys in a lot of other towns. A pot-bellied stove sat in one corner with a coffee-pot bubbling away on top. A few enamel mugs hung on nails in the wall beside the gun-rack. The walls were littered with dodgers, many of them out of date. There were a few chairs, a desk, a filing cabinet. An open doorway led to the lock-ups, and catching sight of the thick iron bars,

Hunter suddenly went cold.

"If . . . ah, if you'll tell me where I can find the mayor . . . ?" he prodded.

"Mr Beecher? sure. Runs the dry-goods store up the street."

Hunter nodded. "Thanks. I'll go look him up."

"Forget it. I'll go fetch him."

"I don't want to — "

"No trouble. His wife'll mind the store."

Left alone, Hunter studied the wanted posters to kill time, trying to ignore the cramping of his guts as he recalled all the years he'd spent with men whose images were on fliers just like these.

Wandering on, he came to the door which led to the cells. There were four of them in all, two on either side of a narrow walkway. Each one was seven feet square, with a bunk, ticking mattress and a blanket. There were no windows in the cells, but there was a small one set high in the wall at the far end of the walkway.

Fortunately the cells were empty right now, so there was no-one around to see Hunter's reaction to the forest of thick iron bars. For the cells brought it all back to him; the five and a half years he himself had spent in Yuma Penitentiary.

His breathing grew heavy as long-suppressed memories began to crowd him. For five and a half years he had been chained to the stone floor of a cell just like these, only his cell had been bigger, nine feet square, and there had been a window too, a window that let in the searing rays of a desert sun hot enough to melt your eyeballs and boil your brains.

Five and a half years chained to a stone floor, allowed to exercise once, twice a month, if that.

He shuddered.

The Pen had held twenty guards and three hundred prisoners. Sometimes the guards watched him from the towers at each corner of the main wall, sometimes from the gate-tower, which also housed the Gatling gun. Sometimes they beat him for no particular reason. It depended on how they felt at the time.

But he'd remained one of the quiet ones, willing to bide his time and wait for someone to notice his good behaviour and set him free.

Only it had been a long wait.

He couldn't even see the four cells in front of him now; he saw only the bars at Yuma. His jaw muscles worked as he relived the bitter hatred and all-consuming lust for revenge which had taken control of him in those early months, and then how he'd cooled off, watching with disgust as other prisoners raced cockroaches to pass the years and talked big of breaking out. He remembered the dull eyes of the men put here for life, for crimes even worse than the one he was supposed to have committed. He shivered.

It was because of those lost souls that he'd become so determined to hold on to his own sanity, working out a number of stupid but suddenly vital mental exercises to keep his feet firmly planted on the ground. *Watch yourself, Hunter. Keep your nose clean. And one day soon, you'll get out of here.*

And he had. Eventually. After five and a half long years, he'd been released. He'd been twenty-one when he went in; now he was pushing thirty. But the flames of revenge still burned within him, every bit as fierce as they had been all those years ago.

But today they were somehow different. Back then, when it had first happened, Hunter's only wish had been to lay his hands on the man who'd framed him for a double killing and stage hold-up he didn't commit and strangle the life out of him. Now he wanted more than just that. He wanted a confession from the real killer; a confession that would prove his innocence once and for all. He wanted that double-crossing sonofabitch Jason Birchell exposed as the murdering scum that he was.

Not even aware of it, Hunter clenched his fists as he recalled the day he'd heard that Birchell had come here to Carver to settle down . . . the day his vengeance-quest had started in earnest.

"Howdy."

He jumped, startled, turned and blinked at the man who was standing behind him, offering his right hand in greeting.

"Name's Clem Beecher," the man went on. "Been looking forward to meeting you, Mr Hunter."

Hunter shoved everything but what was happening now to the back of his mind. He took the mayor's hand and they shook. His interview for the job as town marshal was just about to begin.

2

CLEM BEECHER, the mayor of Carver, was a tall, distinguished-looking man with a thick mane of iron-grey hair and a moustache the same colour beneath a long thin nose and gentle blue eyes. He wore a plain white shirt inside grey pants, a plum-coloured vest and a broad leather belt. He was about sixty or so, his smile easy and open, his direct, friendly manner designed to make Hunter feel more comfortable.

"So," he said as they returned to the outer office. "You're interested in the marshal's job — but you've never done this kind of work before?"

"Nope."

"What makes you think you can do it now?"

Hunter's smile too some of the edge off his reply. "What makes you think that I can't?"

Beecher chuckled, setting his backside against the corner of the paper-littered desk. Over by the stove, Zeb Coulson watched their exchange with open interest.

"Not a thing, Mr Hunter, not a thing. 'Fact, you strike me as being a pretty capable feller altogether. But I'm curious. Not many men of your age or, ah, calibre, figure to settle in a backwater town like this 'un, dodging the odd bullet in between locking up Saturday night drunks, 'specially for the kind of salary we'd be paying. Coffee?"

Hunter shook his head. "No thanks." A bemused smile touched his lips briefly. "If I didn't know better, Mr Beecher, I'd say that you was trying to turn me off this job."

The mayor shrugged. "Don't mean to. Just trying to be straight with you is all. See, if it's excitement you crave, you won't find it here. Oh, Carver's a fine town, don't get me wrong. But it's . . . quietish. For a young feller like you, well . . . it could be boring as hell." He met the younger man's eyes and held them for a long pair of seconds. "Still interested?"

Hunter nodded.

Zeb brought a mug of coffee across to the mayor, who took it and nodded his thanks. "All right," he said, eyeing Hunter keenly. "Tell me something about yourself."

The would-be starpacker sighed, not quite sure where to start. "Well," he said a little self-consciously, "I was born in Lampasas, Texas. Started drifting when I was fifteen or so, not sure why. Just itchy-footed, I guess."

"We all are at that age," Beecher allowed. "Go on."

Hunter shrugged. "I guess I've tried my hand at most things over the years. Did a spell riding herd on a wagon-train bound for Oregon by way of the Columbia Plateau. Rode shotgun for Wells Fargo too, one time. Even had a go at prospecting in California."

"Find any colour?"

"Nary a pinch."

"Too bad. Go on."

Hunter shrugged again. "Well, there ain't much more. Like I said in my wire, I've been working for the J. A. spread down in the Palo Duro Canyon for the last half-year."

The mayor narrowed his eyes. "Charlie Goodnight's outfit?"

"Him and John Adair, yessir. You know Mr Goodnight?"

Beecher shook his head. "Know *of* him, though. Know that he's more'n a mite particular about the men who work for him. Know cattle, do you?"

"Some. Like I said, I'm from Texas."

Beecher's smile formed wrinkles at his eyes and nostrils. "I guess that was a stupid question," he allowed. "Why'd you decide to leave?"

Hunter's sigh was more expressive this time. "I've spent damn' near half my life drifting, Mr Beecher. Decided it was about time I found me a place to set down some roots."

The mayor's calm blue eyes fell to the Frontier Colt in the well-kept buscadero gunbelt around Hunter's hips. "It didn't have anything to do with that, then?" he asked bluntly.

"No sir."

"You know how to use it, though."

"Know how," Hunter replied with a touch of pride. "And more important, know *when*."

Beecher looked impressed. "Sounds like a sensible combination," he said. He studied Tom closely for a moment, and Hunter returned his scrutiny without backing down. After all, everything he'd told the older man was true. He *had* ridden herd on a wagon-train bound for Oregon; signed on as a shotgun guard for Wells Fargo; panned for colour in the California gold-fields. And shortly after coming out of prison, been lucky enough to get a job with the J. A.

"I like you, Hunter," Beecher said

after a pause. "I don't know why. Hell, man, I only met you ten minutes ago. But something tells me you're all right." He took another sip of coffee. "And those references you suggested I check with," he said, referring to John Adair and a few of Hunter's other previous employers, "they speak pretty well of you."

"If it was up to me, I'd take a chance, give you a try. But I can't just go ahead and do whatever I want without I get the agreement of the town council first."

"I understand," Hunter replied.

Beecher scratched at his iron-grey hair. "Truth to tell, boy, this is a kind of unusual situation altogether. Y'see, normally the retiring marshal's deputy would automatically step into his boss's shoes. Only Jake Dabney didn't have a deputy. We were kind of hoping that a local man might step forward, put himself up for election, but that didn't happen. So it'll be up to the town council whether or not you get

31

the job, not the townsfolk themselves. You follow?"

"Yep."

"Right." Beecher smiled, shedding years. "I tell you what we'll do, then. You come by my place tonight, around seven, and I'll introduce you to the other councillors, let them ask you a few questions. Then we'll take a vote on it. That suit you?"

"Sure."

"Good. If the vote goes your way, you'll be taken on as Acting Town Marshal. You do good and you'll be made permanent."

Hunter nodded.

The interview over — at least for the time being — Beecher excused himself to get back to his store. The two men shook, then the mayor left Hunter alone with the fair-haired youngster.

"You did good, Mr Hunter," Zeb said with a grin. "You do as good with the town council tonight and you'll be wearin' the star come sun-up tomorrow."

"'Preciate the confidence," Hunter replied. "And while we're at it, Mr Hunter was my pa. I'd take it kindly if you called me Tom."

"Sure," the boy said, flushing with embarrassment. "I tell you, ah, Tom, happen you get the job, you'll be a mighty welcome sight around here. Been a long couple'a months since we had a starpacker."

"This other feller, Jake Dabney. He retired, huh?"

"Yep," the boy nodded. "Early."

Something in the way he said the word made Hunter's forehead crease. "What happened? Was he ill?"

"Heck no," Zeb replied. "Nothin' like that. Ol' Jake was pushin' fifty and tendin' some towards the gut, but all told I figure he had a pretty easy time of it 'til Jase Birchell come to town an' started his freightin' business. That's when all them roughnecks started comin' in, for the work, y'see, and, well, I guess you know what freighters can be like."

Hunter didn't reply straightaway. Mention of the man who'd framed him all those years before had sent a sharp, distracting tingle across his skin.

"Jake just packed it in," Zeb went on, unaware of the reaction Birchell's name had had on him. "An' I can't really say as I blame him. When you're gettin' along in years, I guess you can do without mixin' it up with the kind'a fellers whose idea of fun is dentin' the marshal's badge with their bullwhips — while said marshal's still wearin' it." He stopped abruptly and looked at Hunter in alarm. "Say, Tom, — I ain't scarin' you off, am I?"

Hunter forced a grin. "Nope," he replied, trying hard to keep the excitement out of his tone. "I was just thinking. Birchell. Seems to me I've heard that name before."

Zeb said, "Maybe you know him. This feller spent quite a while up in Utah an' Wyomin'. Came to settle in Carver 'bout eighteen months ago. They say he made his pile roundin' up stray cattle an' sellin' 'em to the minin' towns just after the War."

"And you say he runs the freight company now?"

"Uh-huh. He the same Birchell you heard of?"

Hunter moved his eyes away from Zeb's innocent young face, unable to lie directly. "Guess not."

"Too bad. You could'a got re-acquainted."

Suddenly anxious to be alone to plan his next move, Hunter made to leave. Zeb, ever helpful, suggested a decent livery for his horse and an inexpensive hotel for him, and with the midmorning sun warm on his back, Hunter led the stallion down-town, deep in thought.

Casey, the bartender at the Oriental Sunset, had identified Ike Daggett and his crew as freighters. That meant that Birchell was Daggett's boss. But what else had the bartender said?

"Boss's outta town on business . . ."

So Birchell was out of town just

now, eh? Hunter allowed himself an arctic smile. He'd have quite a surprise waiting for him when he returned to Carver, then.

But getting even with Birchell wasn't going to be as easy as all that. Hunter clearly remembered the kind of man he'd turned out to be; cold, hard and dangerous. He would have to watch himself every step of the way.

Leaving the roan at the stable, he hefted his saddle-bags over one broad shoulder and headed back towards the two-storey Clarke Hotel. There he booked into a single room, left his things behind the locked door and headed for the barber-shop to get a shave, a haircut and — hopefully — a bath.

It was as he crossed Front Street, dodging wagon and horseback traffic, that he saw the offices of Birchell's freight company.

There was no warmth in him whatsoever as he ran his eyes across the fancy, freshly-repainted shingle.

The trimmed-timber building looked prosperous and opulent. Hunter thought about the old homestead he'd passed through four days earlier and shook his head. While Birchell was living in the lap of luxury, the old widow-woman with the piercing black eyes was living with her beautiful daughter in squalor.

His mouth narrowed down as he continued along the busy main stem.

Birchell had told everyone that he'd made his money rounding up stray cattle and selling them to the beef-starved mining towns just after the War Between the States. Well, that was plausible enough, he supposed. A lot of fellows had made their fortunes that way. But Hunter knew better of Birchell. He knew that Birchell had made *his* fortune robbing a stagecoach and shooting the poor devil in the driver's seat and the young man riding shotgun beside him — and framing a twenty-one-year-old kid for the crime.

Reaching the barber-shop, he stepped

into the scented world beyond the open door. There were two big mirrors, a couple of chairs, shelves with hair tonics and mugs with names on them. A fat man was having a shave in one of the chairs. The barber working on him looked like an immigrant, an Italian or a Greek.

"Good day," he said.

Hunter nodded, took a seat. He watched the barber's deft hands as he scraped stubble from the fat man's face, flicking the excess lather onto a sheet of old newsprint before attacking a new area.

"What will you want, my friend?" the barber asked, moving the cut-throat razor along his customer's top lip.

"Haircut, shave, bath."

"Then you have come to the right establishment. You will want your clothes laundered?"

"That might be an idea."

"I will see to it while you take a bath."

"Obliged."

Hunter sat back, glanced down at a copy of the Carver *Star*, which someone had left on the chair beside him. One glance told him that it was just a couple of pages of births, deaths, marriages and local gossip. He didn't bother to read it.

Shifting his gaze, he caught sight of himself in the mirror ahead. A new question suddenly sprang to mind. Would Birchell remember him when at last they came face to face again? They'd only ever met just the once, and that had been at night, by fire-glow.

In the end he decided that Birchell would probably walk right past him without a flicker of recognition. But Hunter wondered if the man would still remember his name, or indeed, if Birchell could ever forget it. He wondered what the murderer's reaction would be when he found out that the kid he'd double-crossed all those years before was back again, this time behind a tin star.

"Right," the barber said. He'd

cleaned up the fat man and was now indicating the chair for Hunter. Hunter got up, went over and sat in it. He didn't remove his gunbelt or pull it around on his waist to sit more comfortably; he'd learned long ago that his gun was best left where it was.

The sound of the barber's scissors relaxed him. After a while he gave up watching the fellow's reflection and looked down at his covered lap. A few locks of brown hair fell across the white sheet draped over him. He paid them no heed, could no longer even see them.

His eyes were far away. He was remembering. Remembering the events which had led him to this time, this place. This moment of revenge.

He'd been twenty-one years of age; old enough to know better after six years of drifting, and yet just easy-going enough to trust a man he'd met on the trail.

Tom Hunter had carried a heavy .36

calibre Navy Colt in those days, and it was said that if you could draw a Navy Colt fast, then you could draw *any* gun fast.

He'd been camped off the trail somewhere in the Chiricahua Apache country of southern Arizona, a bad place for a *pinda-lik-oyi*, or white man, to be alone. Still, here he was, down on his luck and seriously considering going back home to his folks in Lampasas. He was more than a little bored with his life right then, and, in the shadows of the night with only a small fire and an old nag for company, just a little lonely, too.

It was in that moment that he caught a series of faint, skin-stretching sounds. The sharp click of a horse's hooves; the rustling of disturbed sagebrush. Already spooked by being in such inhospitable terrain alone, Tom drew his Colt, hauled back the hammer, took comfort from the triple click the weapon made coming to full cock.

41

Then —

More vague sounds crept to him across the chilly night air. Louder now. Closer. Tom moved back, away from the meagre light of his fire. His horse, chewing on some bunch grass, whickered softly. Tom, watching the night for any signs of movement, took some comfort from the fact that the approaching horse had shod hooves; something no Indian pony would boast.

So it was a white man out there in the shadows; not that that was any guarantee of safety. There were a lot of unsavoury people to be found on the trail, and —

Catching sight of the man sitting aboard the approaching horse, Tom squinted hard to make out his manner. One hand held the reins, the other was upraised, palm out in the universal sign for peace. He was coming in friendly then — or was he?

Tom still couldn't discern him too well, but from what he could see, the rider was bending forward in the saddle, peering ahead to see if anybody sat around the small fire.

"Hello the camp," the newcomer called softly.

"Who *are* you?" Tom called back, watching the rider straighten up, obviously startled.

"Name's Birchell," he said to the darkness, keeping his gravelly voice low. "Saw your camp-fire from the trail, figured I'd ride in, get a little company. Damn' country's makin' me itchy."

Tom relaxed a little to find a kindred spirit. "See a 'Pache behind every rock, huh?"

The man nodded. "See you had the same feelin'."

Tom came out of the shadows, but did not put the Colt away until Birchell had seen it. Then he said, "All right, come ahead and welcome. Climb down a while."

"Obliged."

Birchell was a couple of inches short of six feet, but with a barrel chest

43

that strained the buttons of his sweaty blue shirt and black vest. He had a Walker .44, a big, heavy weapon like Tom's own, and a Spencer carbine in a saddle-sheath. He came down out of the saddle like a man half his size, and did not come to the fire to accept a mug of java until he had seen to his horse, tethering it near Tom's own.

"Thanks," he said, sipping with relish. "Aaah, that feels better. What do they call you, friend?"

Tom told him.

"Pleased to know you, Tom." Birchell reached across the fire, right hand outstretched. They shook. Birchell was in his early thirties, but his bulk, his hard face and the black-grey hair beneath his flat-brimmed, low-crowned hat, served to make him look older. He had a strange face, all sharp planes; stubbled, brown, lined and trail-wise.

It was his gun that Tom noticed most, however. The old Walker seemed well-used and well-cared-for, and in the uncertain firelight Tom saw grease glistening on its holster; not too much but just enough.

"What you doin' out in the middle o' no-place all by yourself, Tom? No offence, but you seem a mite young to be travellin' alone."

"Been trying to find work," Tom replied.

"Any luck?"

By way of answer, Tom gave a bitter laugh.

"Findin' it hard, huh?"

"You could say that."

"What d'you do?" Birchell asked. "Got a trade?"

"No," Tom said. "I guess I'm just a jack-of-*all*-trades. Do this 'n' that. Anything, so long as the pay's fair and it ain't against the law."

Birchell indicated the Navy Colt. "You seem pretty handy with that thing. Ever hired it out?"

"No sir."

"You should. The pay's right good."

Tom watched the other man take

another long pull at his coffee. "Is that what *you* do?" he asked quietly.

Birchell nodded. "When funds get a little low."

The big man finished his coffee, put the mug down and glanced around him. Like Tom, not once did he stare directly into the fire. To do so, and then look back into the night, would mean to lose precious seconds waiting for his eyes to adjust to the darkness — seconds he couldn't afford if a pack of scalp-hungry Chiricahuas came a-calling.

"You got yourself a right handy little campsite here, Tom. Water just over yonder. Forage for your horse. Uh-huh. Right handy," Birchell noted appreciatively.

"I guess."

The older man shivered. "By Godfrey, it's cold tonight! Care for a swig of somethin' warmin', boy?"

Before Tom could respond, Birchell rose, moved around the fire and went to his horse. After a second or so's rummaging in his saddle-bags, he came back with a bottle of Jim Beam. Grinning, he pulled the cork and offered it to the younger man.

But Tom wasn't so sure. "Don't you reckon we'd be better off keepin' clear heads?" he asked.

Birchell smiled, and the way he smiled seemed to push all other considerations aside. "Hell, you tellin' me you can't hold your liquor, boy?"

Tom stiffened defensively. "No. But — "

"Here's to swimmin' with bow-legged wimmen, then," the other man chuckled, splashing whiskey into both their mugs. "Your health, Tom."

Against his better judgement, Tom tasted the whiskey. It was strong, and its amber fire made him choke a little.

"Don't worry, boy," Birchell told him not unkindly. "Second one always tastes a whole lot better."

Tom took another careful sip.

"You say you're lookin' for work, huh?" Birchell asked.

"Uh-huh."

"I'm on my way to a new job," Birchell said, his low voice sounding like gravel on gravel. "Feller down on the border's havin' a little trouble with his livestock. God-damn renegades from Mexico keep raidin' it."

"He wants some protection, does he?"

"The best," Birchell confirmed, his face splitting with a cold grin. "That's why I got the word." He took another drink. "Sh'd be easy enough. A little line-ridin', a little night-hawkin'. Figure to catch them greasers in the act an' chase 'em all the way down to Mexico City!" He eyed his new-found companion shrewdly. "You want in?" he asked.

The question took Tom by surprise. Birchell saw the look on his face and said, "You look like a smart-enough lad. Handy with a gun, 'telligent. And I figure I'll need some help if them renegades is as feisty as they say."

Tom paused, unsure. "Is it legal?"

he asked cautiously.

"'Course!"

The boy turned it over in his mind. He could sure use the work and the money it would bring him. And Birchell seemed like a decent fellow. All in all, it was mighty tempting. He felt Birchell's eyes on him, and abruptly said, "All right."

They sealed the deal with another drink — or rather, in Tom's case, a sip, which Birchell noted with a scowl.

"Don't kiss it, boy! Take a man-size pull!"

Tom drank more.

"That's the way!" Birchell enthused.

It was true what he'd said. The second drink *did* taste better. And between them, they soon finished the bottle. But afterwards, when he thought back on it, Tom realized that *he* had finished the bottle. For every drink *he* took, Birchell had just wet his lips. He had given the *impression* he was drinking hard and getting as drunk as

Tom, but it was all an act.

After a while Tom passed out. He came awake once, twice, three times, each time feeling sweaty and sick. His mouth tasted bitter and his head felt heavy. He fell back to sleep, promising himself that he'd never touch whiskey again . . .

The next time he opened his eyes, the sky was bright and blue. It was early morning, by the position of the sun. A faint breeze caressed his skin. The sound of crickets came to him as he tried to remember why his head ached so. Then he had it. The whiskey. The whiskey and the man named Birchell. And that was when the crickets stopped their chattering, and Tom realised that something was wrong.

Chiricahuas!

He struggled to sit up, shaking his head to clear it as he reached for the Colt on his hip.

A voice grated, "Hold it right there, you lousy little bastard!"

Tom blinked, looking up. He was surrounded by a group of white men on horseback. Their handguns and rifles were aimed at him with a frightening steadiness.

3

EVEN though his head felt as if it was covered with a heavy blanket, one glance told Tom all he needed to know. This was a posse. And it was hostile.

The men were dressed in a variety of store-bought clothes; woollen shirts, coveralls, corduroy jackets and flat-heeled boots. Townsmen. They stared down at him with hatred in their eyes, and he took scant comfort from the fact that their guns looked as if they hadn't been used for a long time.

There was no movement except for the lazy swishing of a horse's tail every so often. Tom wondered what in hell was going to happen next.

The man who had climbed down from his gelding had a highly-polished star pinned to his woollen shirt and a five-shot double-action .38-calibre

Tranter in one big hand. His face, beneath a wide-brimmed Plainsman hat, was brown and hard, with sneering lips and flared nostrils. For a lawman, Tom thought sourly, he would have made a great outlaw.

"All right, kid — on your feet."

"What's all this — "

"Get up, I said!"

Slowly Tom did as he was told. When he was facing the lawman their eyes locked. The badge-toter pulled Tom's gun from its holster and tucked it into his weapons belt. The Tranter was still aimed at him, almost touching his stomach.

The lawman's brown eyes never left Tom's face as he said, "Norm check his saddle-bags."

Tom tried again. "What *is* this?"

The lawman sniffed. "Did a little celebratin' last night, did you? I can smell the rotgut on you a mile off. Boy, you made a *big* mistake when you opened that bottle."

Tom watched as the others, eleven of

them, dismounted and led their horses to the scrubby bunch grass where his own nag was tethered. They mumbled to one another about how well they'd done, catching the killer and all, and Tom felt a quiver of fear in his belly. Were they talking about *him*?

"Where's Birchell?" he asked abruptly.

The lawman's laugh was short. "Don't come that, boy."

The man who was searching Tom's saddle-bags turned and said, "There's nothin' here."

"All right — where is it?" The lawman's tone told Tom he'd better have the right answers. But he didn't *have* any answers just questions.

"Where's what?"

The lawman put his Tranter away, slowly and deliberately. Then, suddenly, he moved, straightening up quickly and backhanding Tom across the face. He didn't smile and he didn't laugh, just kept the same look of disgust. Tom went back a couple of steps but stayed on his feet. He stared at the lawman as a thin trickle of blood wound its way from between his split lips.

"Where's what?" he asked again, the faintest hint of defiance in his tone.

"The fifteen thousand dollars' worth of silver bullion you killed two men to get at."

Tom sobered up quickly. "*What?*"

"Where is it?"

"This is a mistake — "

"*Where is it?*"

"Now listen, marshal — "

The lawman landed another blow to Tom's faced, harder this time. Tom's jaw went numb. Before he could recover, the lawman punched him in the stomach and he stumbled to his knees.

"What's your name?" the marshal demanded.

Tom bit back an angry retort, sensing that if he behaved rationally he would get a chance to explain. "Tom Hunter," he said quietly.

"Where you from?"

"Out of Hartford." It was a small

town about seventy miles northwest. He'd worked in a store there, doing the fetching and carrying, until he'd grown bored and decided to move on.

"How long you been out on the trail?"

"Three, four weeks."

"What you doin' right in the middle of Injun country?"

"I was just . . . looking for work someplace." Out in the open it sounded feeble, like a quick lie. He felt very small and vulnerable.

"You been down on your luck, right?" The lawman waited until Tom nodded, then said, "So you thought you'd hold up a stagecoach and kill the driver an' his shotgun guard for fifteen lousy grand." The accusation was fired at him like a bullet.

Where was Birchell? Tom felt panic rising, thick and tangible. What about their partnership? Their agreement to ride off and protect some fellow's livestock down on the border?

"Where's the bullion?" the marshal snarled.

Tom's voice was thick with desperation. "Now listen, mar —

"Bury it, did you? Where?"

"I don't know what you're talking about, dammit!"

That got him another stinging backhander. He clenched his puffed lips tight, trying to reason his way out of it. But the same question kept coming back to him. *Where was Birchell?*

Then one of the posse-members spoke up. "Time enough to get the truth out'n him once we're back in town, Mace. Not right here smack-dab in the middle of Injun country."

The lawman paused, and Tom could almost hear his mind turning it over. Then the marshal nodded. "Right, Harvey — throw me that lariat. Norm, you get his horse saddled and ready. We're gonna tie you good and tight, boy. If you know what's good for you, you'll 'fess up to ever'thing before it comes to a trial."

There was a mumble of agreement as most of the men mounted up. The marshal gave orders for three of them to stay behind and search for the bullion, in case Tom had buried it nearby. They obeyed reluctantly, scared — and with good reason — of clashing with the cruel Chiricahua bucks hereabouts.

They threw Tom up into his saddle, arms tied behind his back, the rope stretching out ahead to where the marshal tied it around the saddlehorn. It was a moment Tom would remember in the cold darkness of his time in prison; that feeling of terrible, sinking dread settling into his guts. He sat in silence as they started off, and cast one glance back at his campsite. Then they were on the main trail and he couldn't see it any more. All he could see was the marshal, the posse and the rope. it chafed his wrists. Every so often the marshal yanked on it and nearly pulled him out of the saddle.

How long would it be before the rope

around his wrists became a rope around his neck?

Desperation began to gnaw at his vitals.

Where was Birchell?

There was no sign of him.

Was Birchell his real name?

Tom couldn't say.

All he knew for sure was that a man he'd shared his camp with last night, a man with whom he'd gotten drunk, was now nowhere to be found. And that a posse of hard men were accusing him of a double killing and the theft of a fortune in silver bullion.

It would be pointless to explain what had happened to the lawman riding ahead. But maybe, when they arrived in town, he could make someone listen and believe him. It was a slim hope, sure, but all he had.

The only alternative was a choking, kicking death.

Clean-shaven, bathed, his hair cut and his clothes laundered, Hunter began to relax. He'd spent most of the afternoon watching the water in the tub out back of the tonsorial parlour turn grey as trail-dust came off his skin. He'd also taken a bite to eat at a nearby chow-house and wandered around town, getting to know the layout of the place.

It was around 7 pm when he finally tapped on the double door of Clem Beecher's store and was admitted by Beecher's wife, a homely but still-attractive woman with soft grey hair and warm blue eyes.

The store was much how he'd expected it to be; shelves filled with bolts of silk, linen and lace; pots and pans; a stack of china; some bottles filled with coloured water and jars full of candy. The whole place was as clean as a new pin and the air had a strange but pleasing smell to it, a mixture of all the nice, scented things the Beechers had for sale.

"You'll be Mr Hunter," said Beecher's wife.

"Yes, ma'am."

"Follow me."

She led the way past the counter and through a door at the back of the store. It was cooler now, but still warm enough to make Tom start sweating as they entered the parlour. Beecher was there with five other locals. They all stood up when Hunter came in and Mrs Beecher introduced him.

"Howdy again, Tom," Beecher said, his eyes creasing up as he smiled. "Let me introduce you to these here fine gentlemen who make up our town council."

There was Hobart, the manager of Carver's only bank, a fellow who looked more at home with the figures in his ledgers than with his fellow councillors; Carthy and Smallwood, both storekeepers like Beecher himself, and just as friendly; Greaves, the sharp and immaculate owner of the livery stable in which Tom had left his horse; and Lew Faulkner, owner of the town's second saloon, the Dancing Lady.

Introductions over, they sat down. Tom perched on the edge of his seat and answered their questions as he toyed with his hat.

Hobart was naturally concerned about the security of his bank. Tom told him that he could understand that, and that if he got the job, the bank would be high on his list of places to keep an eye on. Indeed, he stressed the fact that it was in his own interest to do so. "After all," he asked mildly, "if the bank gets robbed, how do I draw my month's pay?"

That made them laugh, and Hobart nodded, apparently satisfied by Tom's quiet confidence.

Faulkner wanted to know Tom's attitude toward saloons.

"You'll get no problems from me," he replied after a moment. "So long as you're careful who you serve, and run straight games of chance."

"You are familiar with the workings of our judicial system, I take it, Mr Hunter?"

"Passably fair, Mr Smallwood. And keen to learn more."

More searching questions followed. Hunter answered them all as best he could. Twenty minutes later he was asked if he'd go wait out in the kitchen whilst Beecher and his colleagues deliberated over his possible appointment. The mayor's wife gave him coffee, cake and idle chatter to help him pass the next anxious quarter-hour.

A short time later Beecher asked him to go back into the parlour. As he complied, his guts began to wind ever tighter.

"Tom," the mayor said once they were all seated again. "We've chewed things over and reached a decision. Town like Carver might be small, might be quiet. But it still needs someone to uphold the law. So . . . " He smiled. "Happen you're serious about settlin' down and makin' a go of it — "

"I am."

"Then you've got the job — on a

two-month trial."

"Congratulations," said Smallwood, shaking him by the hand.

Tom had to fight to keep down the surge of triumph that threatened to overwhelm him. "Thanks. I . . . well, all I can promise you is that I'll do my best — "

"Sure you will," Beecher said confidently. He took a six-pointed tin star from one vest pocket and handed it over. A few minutes later Tom was handed the Beecher family Bible and sworn into office.

"Welcome to Carver, boy," the mayor said sincerely.

Hunter smiled. It felt good to *belong*.

The following morning he arrived early at the law office.

As he closed the door softly behind him, he saw that Zeb Coulson was curled up in the chair behind the desk, asleep. Looked like the kid had been staying here twenty-four hours a day. Well, all that would change now. There'd be no need for him to hold the fort all by himself any more.

Hunter went to the stove and put some coffee on to boil. He couldn't shuck the feeling of how strange it seemed to be wearing a star. Town Marshal Tom Hunter. It sounded fine. But he couldn't kid himself. It was only temporary, until justice was done. Then he'd be moving on again, drifting like he always had.

He peered out the window into the slowly-brightening street. He didn't *want* to move on. As he had told Beecher, the desire to set down roots had grown increasingly strong within him. But it was inevitable. After all, how would Beecher react when he discovered that Tom had only pinned on the badge to settle his own scores? As far as the mayor was concerned, Tom was a man who wanted only to put down roots and work hard. Once he got his confession from Birchell, however, the game would be up. Beecher would realise he'd been told a pack of lies by an ex-con just to get a job through which he could gain revenge. That Tom would, in the process, prove himself innocent was immaterial. What would matter most to a man like Beecher was that he had been betrayed by a man to whom he had given his friendship and trust.

Hunter heard a noise behind him and turned around. Zeb was sitting up and stretching. The boy's eyes suddenly opened wide as he saw the star on Tom's shirt-front.

"Uh . . . mornin', *marshal!*"

"Mornin', Zeb," the older man replied. "And it's Tom, remember?"

"Sure. Tom. So — you got the job, huh?"

"Uh-huh."

"Congratulations."

"Thanks."

"Hell, look at me. I'm a mess. Give me a couple minutes to get washed up." Zeb got to his feet, stretched again and hurried off to someplace out back. Tom, momentarily alone, looked around the office. He allowed himself a smile. The kid's enthusiasm must be rubbing off on him. For once he was looking forward to the day ahead. And, who knew —

But no. There was no point to making his mind up about the future. He would take the cards as they were dealt, and make the best of them whichever way they fell. He didn't really have a lot of choice.

After coffee, he and Zeb patrolled the town, making small-talk and getting to know each other. The boy introduced him to several citizens as they strolled along the boardwalk, and by the time they got back to the office a lot of ice had been broken. During the morning, Ed Judd, the editor of the Carver *Star*, stopped by to ask Tom a few details about himself for a special edition of the paper. Remembering that Jason Birchell had a financial interest in the *Star*, he gave guarded answers to Judd's questions, determined to give nothing away that might forewarn Birchell that he was the same Tom Hunter from all those years before.

Come lunchtime, he and Zeb dined on ham, eggs, grits and coffee, which Zeb brought over from the diner across the street. Then they sat and talked for a while about the town and its inhabitants.

For the most part, it seemed that they were a peaceable lot. Most of the trouble came from Jason Birchell's freighters. Although they were all from the hard breed, Ike Daggett was harder than most and, as such, had incurred the hatred of most Carver townsfolk. The citizens didn't take kindly to the rough-and-ready freighters, but, realising that Birchell had money to invest in their town, determined to live with them in an uneasy peace.

Some time during the afternoon, Clem Beecher poked his head around the office door to see how Tom was settling in. Tom told him he was doing fine.

The rest of the day passed without incident.

That evening, as the dying sun painted the sky a breathtaking orange-pink, Hunter pulled on his hat and went to the door.

"See you in a while, Zeb. Just doing the rounds."

Zeb had been cleaning a couple of rifles from the rack on the wall. "Want me to come along?"

"That's okay. You're more important right here."

It was cooler now. A rare breeze picked up sand and sent it swirling down the street in a series of miniature dust-devils. Over at the bank, Hunter saw a light burning in Hobart's office. He looked right and left, then crossed toward the grey stone building.

Tapping lightly at the double doors, he waited for a couple of seconds before Hobart pulled back one of the shades to peer out. The bank manager's frown lasted only until he saw Tom's badge.

Then he smiled, unlocked the door and opened up.

"Good-evening, marshal."

Tom touched the brim of his hat. "Mr Hobart. You're working late, I see. Everything all right?"

"Fine, thank you. Sometimes bank business has little respect for one's home life, and demands to be settled immediately."

"So I've heard."

"How was your first day on the job?"

"Just fine, thanks." Hunter let out his breath. "Well, so long as everything's in order . . ."

"It is, marshal. But thank you for coming across to make sure."

"That's what the job's all about. Goodnight."

"Goodnight."

Tom moved along the sidewalk. It was getting darker by the minute now, and the streets were almost empty. Tom heard the muted sounds of a piano coming from the Dancing

Lady, a dog yapping somewhere in the darkness at the edge of town. He thought of Beecher, Zeb, some of the people he'd met during the course of the day, and felt at home.

Then —

A scream knifed through the night air.

He pin-pointed it straightaway. Uptown, and on his left. The Oriental Sunset.

No more than a second or two after the scream ended, Tom began moving with long, purposeful strides, preparing himself for whatever had happened — or what was *about* to happen.

Yellow light spilled from above and beneath the saloon's batwings, falling in a warm puddle on the boardwalk outside. As he pushed through the curious rubber-neckers who had gathered to see what was going on, Tom sensed the quietness from within the place. It was eerie. Saloons were never built for silence. They should be filled with gaiety, music, fun. Without any of that they were somehow incomplete, and more like undertakers' parlours.

He pushed through the batwings, stopped just inside the doorway and took in the situation at once.

She was a good-time girl, you could see that. She was in her late twenties, perhaps a bit older beneath all that rouge. Even so, she didn't deserve to have a big yellow-blue bruise across her left cheek. Tom winced as he saw it; the bruise and the tears making her face shine.

She was halfway between the bar and the batwings, and she was on her knees. If it hadn't been for the man standing over her, clutching one thin arm, she would have collapsed in a heap.

Tom's eyes travelled up to him, slowly.

He was big, rough and bearded, but it wasn't Daggett or anyone he'd been with yesterday, even though he had *freighter* stamped all over him.

"All right — what's going on?" Tom

demanded. He stood with his legs slightly apart, well-balanced, hands at his sides, stock-still. His eyes panned from left to right, covering all the patrons, then came back to the man and the sobbing girl in the centre of the big, smoke-hazy room.

The big, barrel-chested man was sweating. He studied Tom through drunken, bloodshot eyes. Tom returned his stare levelly. "I asked you what was going on," he repeated.

There was a pause. Tension thickened in the air. Then, after what seemed like forever, the big man nodded once, twice, another couple of times.

"I'll tell ya what's goin' on. You see her?" He yanked the girl roughly to her feet and she let out another cry. "She thought she was too good for me, wouldn't have a drink with me, go someplace and have a little fun."

The girl looked up, and just for a moment her courage broke through. "That's right! I *wouldn't* go with him! Sure, I might be a sportin' girl, marshal, but everyone knows about *him*!"

"What about him?" Tom asked quietly.

"Shut up, you lyin' bitch!"

"Let go of her arm and let her speak!" Tom told the freighter. He didn't have to add a threat. The big man could see the way Tom's right hand hung close to his Frontier Colt clearly enough, even through his drunken stupor. He took his time about it, but eventually he released his grip on the girl and muttered a curse.

The girl rubbed her arm where he'd gripped it, her bottom lip quivering. But still she managed to blurt out, "He . . . he *hurts* girls, marshal. That's how he gets his fun. He'll give 'em a couple of dollars an' sweet-talk 'em . . . but then he . . . he beats 'em up, takes his m — money back!"

"You lyin' — "

"Everybody knows it!"

The muscles in Tom's jaw worked as he glanced at the saloon's two bartenders, neither of whom was known to him. "That true?" His grey eyes scanned their round, scared faces.

The older bartender, casting a frightened glance at the freighter, shook his head. He seemed to shake it too quickly. "That ain't true, no sir, marshal. The girl's lyin', jus' like he says."

"You're willing to say that on oath when the circuit judge comes 'round?"

"Well . . ." The bartender gulped nervously.

Tom returned his attention to the freighter. "All right, mister. Unbuckle your Colt. You're coming over to the jail."

The big man grinned coldly.

"Come on," Tom snapped. He pointed to the percentage girl. "Someone take care of her. I'll want to see her in my office first thing in the morning."

"Hey now, listen here, starpacker . . ."

The big freighter took one step forward, but the look in Tom's eyes made him pause before turning one into two. "No; you listen here. You might frighten all these other folks, but you don't scare me. I've been hired to keep law and order in this town, and as far as I'm concerned, you've just broken the law. So unbuckle that gun, or I'll come across and unbuckle it for you."

The freighter glared at him. He returned the stare unflinchingly. Around them, the silence was electrifying, until a voice off to Tom's right said, "Hang on there, starpacker. That's Bill Tanner you're talkin' to. He's a good man. I can't allow you to take 'im off to jail for the night. Why, he's due out with a shipment for Tucson come sun-up."

Tom turned slowly, his lips compressed.

Surrounded by his cronies, Ike Daggett stood up and grinned mirthlessly. All at once, a new tension filled the air.

4

HE must have been sitting back in the shadows of a corner table, just waiting for the right moment to speak.

Well, Tom thought, he'd sure as hell picked it. And now Daggett sauntered around a couple of other tables until he stood towering above Tom, and as he looked down at the marshal, his cocksure grin was as wide as ever.

"Be reasonable, starpacker. Bill's got a shipment bound for Tucson first thing tomorrow. Let him enjoy himself tonight, will you?"

When he replied, Tom's voice was low and deep. "Get out of my way, Daggett. Don't get involved. Tanner — I'm not going to say it again. Take off that weapons belt and get *over* here!"

Daggett turned to address the

saloon's other patrons. "Hear that?" he asked in an injured voice. "This is our new marshal, huh? Looks like all that power's gone to his head, am I right?"

His friends mumbled agreement.

"'Course, you don't *like* lawmen, do you?" Tom said casually. "You like poking fun at 'em, the way I hear it. 'Specially when they're getting on in years and running to fat." He was thinking of Marshal Dabney, and what Zeb had told him about Birchell's freighters denting his badge with their heavy bullwhips.

Daggett looked as if he was about to spit, but then changed his mind. "You're right, starpacker," he allowed. "I *don't* like lawmen. Don't like 'em any more'n I like snot-nosed little cowboys." He smiled coldly. "In fact, you could say I downright dee-*spise* 'em!"

Tom saw it coming a mile off. He knew Daggett was planning something underhand by the way he moved his right shoulder back as he kept talking.

When the punch came, then, he was ready for it.

It was a big, meaty fist. Just the kind of fist you'd expect a man like Daggett to have. And if it had connected, Tom would have gone down and woken up sometime tomorrow. But it didn't connect. Tom stepped back, dodged it and sent his own right fist slamming into Daggett's belly. The shock of the blow sent a sharp pain up his right arm.

He heard the breath come out of Daggett's mouth and smelled its rotten sourness. If he knew anything at all about fighting, then it was to put a man like Daggett down quickly.

So he did.

Even as Daggett doubled up, Tom bunched his right fist and jabbed as hard as he could, ignoring the smarting of his knuckles as the fist caught Daggett's chin and lifted him back up.

A thin worm of blood trickled from

one of Daggett's split lips. He reached out to grab Tom but he was winded and slow, and Tom knew he had to press his advantage before the bigger man recovered enough to trap him between those thick arms.

He threw another punch at Daggett's exposed belly, felt his fist sink in, then followed it up once, twice to the face, watching as Daggett gave a grunt and fell backwards, hitting the floorboards hard. He lay there, struggling feebly, and as Tom watched, his eyes glazed and closed. Tom took a deep breath to steady himself against the heady rush of adrenalin.

"Now — "

"*Marshal!*"

Tom whirled around just as Tanner, taking advantage of the momentary lull, grabbed for his gun.

Tom reacted instantly.

His right fist closed around the wooden grips of his Frontier Colt. His index finger slipped through the trigger-guard and his thumb came up over the hammer. By the time he'd pulled the gun from its holster, he'd hauled back the hammer, felt the trigger click forward once, twice, three times. Then he squeezed the trigger and the weapon roared.

In all, it took about half a second.

There was no time for fancy shooting. Few marksmen, even the best, could wing a man intentionally. That kind of shooting only took place in dime novels.

Tom's bullet took Tanner in the chest, up high so that when he toppled backwards, the hole, leaking crimson, started to look like a red necktie before he hit the floor. He sprawled in the sawdust, breathing noisily, his head propped against the brass foot-rail in front of the bar.

His breathing filled the room for a couple more seconds.

Then it stopped.

Tom quickly scanned the room to make sure there would be no more trouble. Although he felt trembly inside, his movements were steady as he pulled back the handgun's hammer, turned the cylinder, flipped out the spent shell and replaced it with a live round from one of the loops on his belt.

The Colt back in its holster, he bent and hauled the half-conscious Daggett to his feet. Daggett was moaning and his eyes were now partly open but squinted, as if the light from the kerosene lanterns above were too bright for him.

He said awkwardly, "My . . . my jaw . . . it's broke . . ."

Tom was too angry to reply. Instead he shoved the bigger man roughly through the batwing doors and out into the night. He heard the sudden rush of excited conversation start up inside the saloon. Outside he spied Zeb, Beecher, Hobart and Ed Judd among the spectators on the boardwalk. They wanted to ask him what had happened, he could tell, but the look on his face as he pushed the stumbling

Daggett across Main Street must have warned them off.

He took no pleasure in killing. And maybe Bill Tanner's death could have been avoided if only Daggett hadn't started a ruckus. Tom's lips narrowed to a grim line as all his fury became directed at the hulking figure before him.

Later on, things somehow got organised.

Zeb arranged for Jack Flowers, the town mortician, to stretch Tanner out and bury him. Money found in Tanner's pockets would pay for the burial, and whatever was left over could go to the saloon-girl, by way of compensation.

Daggett was thrown into one of the cells, and eventually Doc Porter, a spotlessly clean and friendly individual, was called in. He examined Daggett briefly, assured him that his jaw was *not* broken, and painted Tom's grazed knuckles with iodine before binding them.

Tom sat quietly in the outer office for a long time afterwards, with Zeb and Clem Beecher for company. He wondered how the events of the evening would change his situation, both as town marshal and vengeance-seeker. He'd killed one of Birchell's employees. He'd arrested Birchell's foreman. Would those facts in any way change the plans he had to get Birchell's confession?

After a time, Beecher broke in on his thoughts. "How are you feeling now, Tom?"

The troubled lawman glanced up. "All right."

"You sure?"

"Uh-huh."

"There was no way 'round it, way I hear folks tell it. You *had* to kill him."

Tom shifted, sitting up straighter in his creaky Douglas chair. "Yeah, I had to. But maybe if Ike Daggett had kept out of it, Tanner might not have made a play for his iron." His voice sounded old and cracked in the late-night stillness, and the words came out as if they had been said again and again, which indeed they had — in his mind.

Beecher stood up, sighing. "You could say 'maybe' about so many things, Tom. But no matter how many times you say it, you'll never get to change what's already happened."

"I know." Tom also got to his feet. There was no point in discussing it further. It was history now. "I'll see you tomorrow," he said pointedly.

Beecher stepped out into the shadows and soon his footsteps were lost in the darkness. Tom studied his young deputy. "Go on home," he said tiredly. "You've done enough for one day."

"Heck, I don't mind st — "

"*Starpacker!*"

They paused for a moment as Daggett's voice came from the lock-ups. Tom said, "Go on home, Zeb." He threw a glance over his shoulder, toward the cells. "Hang on, Daggett,

I'll be with you in a minute." When he turned back, Zeb still stood in the centre of the room, undecided. "Go on, Zeb. That's an order. I can manage here."

After Zeb left, Tom went through to the back of the jail and stood inside the doorway, watching the big freighter glare at him through the bars of the cell. Daggett looked even more like an animal now, but maybe it was just his surroundings that made him seem so.

"What's the matter?"

Daggett nodded toward the cell door, wincing at the action. "That," he said flatly. "Open it up."

"Why?"

"Ah, don't get smart, starpacker. Open up. You ain't got no reason to hold me here an' you know it."

"I'd call attacking the town marshal reason enough."

"What attack?" Daggett asked with a raspy laugh. "I never laid a finger on you."

"Maybe. But there's plenty of

witnesses to say that you tried."

"Hell, if anyone should be locked up, it's you, the way you murdered poor ole Bill Tanner." Daggett paused; then, seeing that his jibe had had no effect, he began to pursue another line of thought. "Come on, marshal. Open the goddam door and we'll say no more about it. All right, so you killed Bill. What the hell? Maybe he deserved it. Some fellers go through their whole lives just born to die. Listen. Maybe you don't know, but I'm foreman of the Birchell Freight Company. When Mr Birchell gets back to town, he ain't gonna take too kindly to you when he finds out you're keepin' me locked up here for no good reason." He smiled, but through that beard it was difficult to distinguish it from a sneer. "Let me out an' I'll smooth things over with the boss about Bill Tanner. Otherwise it'll go hard for you."

Innocently, Tom asked, "He can be a hard man, then, can he, this Birchell?"

"The hardest," Daggett confirmed. "Second to me."

"When's he due back in town?"

Certain that he was winning now, Daggett said, "Tomorrow afternoon sometime."

Tom smiled briefly. "Well, if he wants you, he'll have to come and get you. But that might be tricky, cause you ain't leaving here until you've been seen by the circuit judge."

"*Hell*, starpacker!" Daggett flew off his bunk and grabbed at the bars with his meaty fists. "Judge comes to town last Thursday of ever' month! That's three weeks away!"

"That's tough," Tom said harshly as he turned away.

"Birchell'll make you pay!" Daggett screamed.

Tom went back into the main office, locking the door to the cell-block behind him. It had been a long and tiring day. He went over to the lamp hanging from the beam which ran across the centre of the ceiling, turned it down low, flopped back into his chair and wearily lifted his boots to the desk's edge. On the wall, the old yellow-faced clock chimed midnight.

It all seemed to catch up with him now; his first day in a new and unfamiliar job; patrolling the streets; the fist-fight; the gunfight. He closed his eyes, expecting nightmares, but there was nothing save darkness.

At first.

The nightmares came later, as his breathing grew deeper and he slept.

The nightmares of his past.

The stagecoach driver's name had been John McGiff. He was sixty-five years old and his face was brown and wrinkled like old leather. His eyes were still a clear blue, however, and his hair, although silver, was thick. He was a man of quick wit and rich, deep laughter. It was true that he'd started walking with a stoop these past six or seven months, but when the sun was high overhead and he shucked out of his canvas jacket and rolled up the sleeves of his sweat-stained, red-check shirt, you could see by the thickness of his arms that he was still in good shape, used as he was to handling the big green Concord coach and its six-horse team of leaders, swings and wheelers.

His shotgun guard, by contrast, was almost completely his opposite. Frank Kelso was twenty-three. He had dark-brown hair, a light rash of freckles and bright brown eyes. He was good-looking and easy-going, and had been riding shotgun now for almost five months. Like McGiff, he was a well-liked and now-familiar sight along the stage route. He carried a twelve-gauge Greener beneath his seat up on the box beside the driver, and just recently had taken to chewing tobacco, spending more time aiming his spit at passing mesquite bushes than keeping his eyes skinned for trouble.

This particular stretch, however, though lonely and littered with cholla and tall grass which could provide would-be road-agents with ample cover, was not known as a black-spot. Two miles up ahead sat a way-station, and seven miles beyond that lay the town of Hogan, which was named after the huts made by the Navajo Indians who used to live there.

On the day that was destined to be the last of their lives, the temperature was way up, squeezing big drops of sweat from the driver and guard and making their clothes stick uncomfortably to their bodies. Inside the coach there were only three passengers, a young woman and her baby daughter and an old, bow-legged rancher named Brandon. In the strong-box beneath the driver's seat there was fifteen thousand dollars' worth of silver bullion.

And on the trail ahead —

"*Whoa!*"

John McGiff pushed down hard with his right foot, kicking on the brake. The wheels locked as he hauled on the ribbons, creating a cloud of dust around the coach as it slewed to a halt. The jingling of harness, the pounding of hooves, the faint, dry creak of the coach's ageing suspension; they were all gone now, and the air was quiet.

One of the horses whinnied, stamping as she smelled the fast-congealing blood on the chest of the Indian who lay sprawled across the trail ahead of them.

Flies buzzed over the gory wound, but the Indian — a Chiricahua — just stared unseeing up at the sky. He'd been shot once, and he was dead.

That was when McGiff and Kelso both had the same thought. Were there any more of them lurking about? Their eyes darted to left and right, and Kelso bent forward to reach for the Greener. Inside the coach, the old rancher demanded to know what was going on. The baby, waking up now that the coach had stopped rocking, began to cry.

"Nothin' to fret on," McGiff called down. To Kelso he muttered, "Cover me, son. I'm goin' to shift that red carcass out'n the way."

Although his throat was dry. Frank Kelso managed to keep his voice on an even pitch. "All right, John. Be careful — and be *quick*."

The weight of the Greener in his hands calmed him down a little. It was a formidable weapon, loaded with two rounds of Double-O Buck. Up close, those eighteen pellets could do a lot to discourage a pack of scalp-hungry redskins — he hoped.

McGiff climbed down with smooth ease, his eyes moving all the while. He had left the reins tied around the brake handle, and as he moved along the line of horses he spoke softly to them, stroking their magnificent, glistening bodies to calm them. As he approached the corpse, the flies rose up like a black cloud and flew away.

"By cracky, he stinks," McGiff muttered, bending to take a firm grip under the buck's armpits.

"Hurry up, John. I'll feel better when

we're movin' again."

"Hold on, now, Frankie boy. Won't take but a minute."

And then the brush exploded outward, and a rider burst through onto the trail in front of the coach.

McGiff jumped back, startled. Kelso aimed the shotgun. But then he saw that the man on the horse was white, and that made him pause before squeezing the triggers.

For Kelso, the pause made all the difference between living and dying. The man on the horse lifted a pistol to shoulder-height, took quick, professional aim and shot him in the chest.

"*Frank!*" The name was wrenched from McGiff.

Inside the coach, the woman screamed in fear and the baby sobbed even louder. The old rancher said, "What the hell — ?"

Outside, Frank went backwards, the small of his back hitting the roof of the coach hard, the force of it jerking his hands so that he discharged the Greener's barrels into the warm air. He came forward then, like a rag doll, and fell sideways off the box, landing in a crumpled heap by the bright yellow left-side front wheel.

Defiance came from McGiff in a roar. "You *bastard!*" He was able to take one step forward before the man on the horse turned the barrel of the revolver on him and fired again.

McGiff groaned softly in pain as the bullet punched him to the ground. Dust rose lazily and settled back over him. Blood trickled over the bridge of his nose, staining his left eyebrow.

"All right, you folks in the coach! Stay right where you are and you won't get hurt!"

From inside the coach, the old-timer said, "You ain't gonna harm this woman and child no-how, you goddamned — "

The sound of horse's hooves on dry earth silenced him. He stared at the young woman, whose eyes were shining with hopeless tears. The baby cradled in her arms shifted irritably, stretching and yelling for comfort. The old rancher leaned forward and stroked the baby's head, whispering, "Hold on, missy. Jest hold on."

Outside, the flies began buzzing again, and the rider paused just beyond their vision. Heavy breathing came to their straining ears, as though the rider were exerting himself. Then they caught the sound of metal scraping along wood. The old rancher looked grim as he fought the urge to take a look-see at what was going on just beyond the window. What was it the bandit had said? "Stay where you are and you won't get hurt." What the fellow meant was that he'd kill anyone who saw him.

Wisely, then, the rancher stayed put. Half a minute later the horse's hooves were heard pounding away, and soon were lost altogether. Only the sound of feasting flies disturbed the shimmering air.

They stayed in the coach, sweating as they stared at each other. At last, the rancher — never one to be inactive for long — said, "Hang on, ma'am. I'm goin' — "

"No! Please!"

"That owlhoot's probably long gone by now, an' I got to see if I can do anythin' for the driver'n guard."

Rather than be left alone in the coach, the woman got out with him, turning away quickly when she caught sight of the bodies. She started rocking the baby and talking nonsense to calm it — and herself.

The rancher looked at the dead Chiricahua for a couple of seconds, puzzling over his presence, then went to the driver. His face was carved in grim lines as he watched the flies moving over the bullet-hole in McGiff's forehead. Then he turned to examine the shotgun guard.

"Hey! This yonker . . . he's still alive!"

Incredibly, Frank Kelso was breathing,

albeit in painful gasps. The rancher picked him up gently, carrying him to the door of the coach. Somehow he managed to get him inside.

There was plenty of room to stretch him out on one side of the benches, and seeing the boy again shivering with reaction or fever, the rancher threw his jacket over him. As far as he could make out, the boy had been shot in the right side, almost smack in the belly.

Without consideration of his own advanced years, the rancher dragged the Indian off the trail and hauled the corpse of John McGiff up onto the roof of the coach. Then he went to the woman and put a paternal arm around her. "How's the baby?" he asked gently.

"She . . . she's almost asleep a . . . again."

"Good. Come on, ma'am. That there shotgunner needs a sawbones right bad. He's half-asleep himself now, so if you don't mind ridin' in the coach with him . . ."

The rancher waited until the woman and child were safely installed in the coach, then clambered up onto the box, took the reins, kicked off the brake and started the stage off at an easy pace.

As soon as they reached their destination, word spread fast. A bandit had stolen the strong-box from the Hogan-bound stage. What was in it? Bullion. *Silver* bullion. Fifteen thousand dollars' worth! What about John McGiff and Frank Kelso? John was dead, and Kelso . . . well, he was over at Doc Murphy's surgery. The Doc had removed the bullet from his guts but it could still go either way.

Who would tell McGiff's wife what had happened? Marshal Burroughs had already sent someone. He'd fixed up a posse, too, and they were riding out straightaway. As near as the old rancher could tell, reading the tracks, the posse was looking for one man alone.

The rest was history. The posse had picked Tom up and taken him in. They were convinced that he had robbed the stage. Only he knew otherwise — he and the shotgunner, Kelso. When *he* regained consciousness, he'd give them a description of the real outlaw, and if Tom knew anything about it, that description would fit Jason Birchell.

The marshal's name was Mace Burroughs. He flatly refused to listen when Tom tried to recount the events of the previous night. The lawman was convinced he'd caught the right man. His only line of questioning was to ask where Tom had hidden the bullion.

The bullion.

There were a hundred or more places Birchell could have hidden it. And he could wait for as long as he liked before digging it up and turning it into hard cash. But it was pointless trying to get that through the marshal's thick skull. *Face it*, Tom told himself bleakly, *Birchell's set you up good and proper*.

Oh, sure; there was no hard evidence against him. But there was nothing *for* him, either. His only hope was the shotgun guard. Once *he'd* told them whatever he could, they'd know they'd arrested the wrong man.

But the shotgun guard didn't pull through.

He died in the early hours of Tom's second morning in jail.

The news hit Tom like a punch in the kidneys. It left him numb and hopeless. Now more than ever he could picture himself turning blue and kicking at the end of a rope. The thought left him dry-mouthed and queasy.

He forced himself to hold on to one last shred of hope. Birchell hadn't set him up just to let him hang, had he? No, he couldn't be that callous. More likely he'd set him up just to slow the posse down. And by the time *they* woke up to the fact that they'd arrested the wrong man, Birchell and the bullion would be long gone. The Hogan lawman would realise his error, apologise and set Tom free.

Wouldn't he?

One of the three men the marshal had

left at Tom's campsite came galloping into town late on the second afternoon. Tom pressed close to the bars of his cell, waiting anxiously for the news. He heard the door to the office open, the sound of boots clattering on floorboards, and then the voice of the marshal. "What's up, Nels? What is it?"

"This."

There was a pause. Tom pressed even closer to the bars.

"Hot-damn." The marshal seemed pleased about something. "Where'd you find it?"

"Buried just near where he'd tethered his nag." There was a grim laugh. "He didn't even bury it proper. Left one corner pokin' up outta the ground."

"Empty," the marshal said.

"Yeah. But we found this."

Another pause.

"Good work, Nels. Go on back, keep lookin'."

Tom stood listening, palms clammy. Then the marshal appeared, carrying in one hand a small, oblong box. It was made of metal, and the metal was crusted with powdery earth. In his other hand was what had once been a lock. Now it was twisted and wrenched out of shape; the kind of shape a bullet might make, blasting it open. Burroughs smiled coldly.

"This here is what we call evidence, Hunter. Tells us damn-near ever'thin' we want to know. How you shot the lock off the box, hid the silver someplace, buried the strong-box. Only we found it. Now — you gonna confess to it all and save the county some money? Might go easier on you when you come to stand trial."

The words spilled out of him. "You've got to believe me, marshal! I don't know where the silver's hidden. I didn't have anything to *do* with it!"

"Caesar's ghost, boy, can't you get it into your head? We'll find the bullion sooner or later, and when we do, it's gonna be classed as even harder evidence against you than this here strong-box! If you confess and sign a statement, you might get away with a life sentence."

"But I didn't have anything to *do* with it! Look, at least *try* to find Birchell. *He's* the one you want!"

The marshal shook his head. "Save it. We all know you're guilty. John McGiff was well-known in these parts. Well-known and well-liked. You did the wrong thing when you picked on him an' Frank Kelso."

The marshal left him alone again, and with a pitiful groan Tom sank down onto his bunk, his fists clenched in frustration. *Birchell!* He saw the man's face in his mind, remembered all the smooth talk and the whiskey . . .

What was it that rider had said about the strong-box? "*He didn't even bury it proper. Left one corner pokin' up outta the ground.*"

That was when he realised that Birchell had deliberately set him up to take the rap. All question of Birchell having framed him just to slow the posse down was now gone. Tom knew with fresh understanding that Birchell had deliberately left one end of the strong-box protruding from the earth so that the posse would discover it and be more convinced than ever that they'd caught the right man.

Birchell didn't want to slow the posse down. He wanted them off his back altogether. And he was willing to let an innocent kid hang to get it.

Tom felt the bile rising in this throat. The cell seemed to crowd in on him.

He was lost.

The judge was a yellow-skinned man with close-cropped grey hair and a wart on his right cheek. He had watery blue eyes and sat scribbling notes throughout the trial. Only occasionally did he question the evidence, such as it was. In summing up, he said,

"This is a hard case to judge. On the one hand, there are certain facts we must consider; that one man committed this crime, and only one man was found in the vicinity, a man who was inebriated, as if from some form of celebration, a boy who has admitted to Marshal Burroughs here that the revolver he carried had been used by him to take human life on more than one occasion, albeit in the defence of a claim he was working in the California gold-fields.

"We also have the evidence of the empty strong-box and the lock that was blasted from it. These items were buried — albeit clumsily — beneath the loose soil around the boy's campsite. We assume he buried the stolen loot at a different location, since it hasn't turned up yet, despite an extensive search.

"However, on the other hand, we have this boy's version of what happened. It must be pointed out that no tracks were found at the campsite to suggest the presence of a second man and his mount, although, in fairness to the accused, this observation is fairly academic now, since the eleven upright citizens who formed the posse churned up the earth upon their arrival at the scene.

"The man referred to as Jason Birchell — the man the accused blames for the robbery and murder — is, we have been told by the prisoner, a top gunslinger. If that is the case, then he would almost certainly be known to the authorities. A thorough check, however, has revealed nothing, no mention or description of anyone like him.

"Naturally, if what the boy says is true, then the man could have used an alias. However, we must remind ourselves as to the lengths condemned men will go to cheat the noose."

The judge paused, swallowing. His face was grim and he blinked slowly a couple of times before saying, "The decision as to whether or not the accused is lying rests with you members of the jury. I can only direct you to reach your verdict according to the evidence you have heard."

It was three-fifteen in the afternoon

when the jury — all locals who stared at Tom with open hatred — went out. The heat was oppressive, the mutterings of the townsfolk crowded into the county courthouse ominous. The jury came back fifteen minutes later.

They found him guilty.

Tom felt a noose whip out suddenly from his imagination and tighten around his throat. The judge sat back slowly. He was clearly dissatisfied with the verdict. Marshal Burroughs grinned at Tom. Tom shivered.

The judge said, "I can't help but think that the members of the jury have been influenced in their judgement by the fact that they all knew and liked the stagecoach driver and his guard. Still, there's not many folks hereabouts who *didn't* know and like them. They were as familiar to this district as the sun or the moon, and just as welcome, so I guess we'd have been hard-put to find a completely impartial jury anyway.

"Personally, however, I don't believe that any of the evidence we've heard here this past week proves that the accused *is* guilty, just in the same way that there's been nothing much to prove him innocent. Maybe he's done a good job of lying, leaving me room in my own mind for doubt. Maybe not. Maybe he *did* kill John McGiff and Frank Kelso. Maybe he *did* take the bullion away and secrete it somewhere." His sigh was audible. "I don't know. But justice is justice. *You* have found him guilty, and *I* must punish him.

"Thomas Hunter, I am not going to sentence you to hang. If I thought for one moment that you were guilty of this crime, you would most certainly swing from a high gallows. But my conscience tells me that I should give you the benefit of the doubt.

"Instead, then, I sentence you to ten years' hard labour in Yuma Penitentiary. Should any evidence be forthcoming that might be beneficial to you, then rest assured, you will not be forgotten. Otherwise, you will serve this term in prison for the crime which you may — or may *not* — have committed."

Tom sagged.

So that was it. Ten years in Yuma, and not the hangrope. But there was scant comfort in it. Tom had heard stories about the Pen. Perhaps it would be better to hang and have done with it.

But no; while he still lived there was a chance. A chance, no matter how slim, that he could yet put his hands around Jason Birchell's throat and make him pay.

Marshal Burroughs and one of his deputies took him by the arms and marched him down the centre aisle. His footsteps echoed around the big, oak-panelled room. He felt the townsfolk glaring at him, but couldn't meet their eyes. Their hatred felt like a wild animal about to leap on him.

Just before they reached the courthouse door, a woman stood up and looked at him through piercing, coal-black eyes.

She was in her mid-sixties, her grey hair tied in a bun above her tanned and wrinkled face.

"*Murderer!*" she whispered, and there was a terrible force in the way she said it. Hunter went cold.

"Calm down now, Mrs McGiff," said a prim-looking woman who had been seated beside her.

McGiff!

So the woman with the black eyes had been the stagecoach driver's wife — and now was his widow . . .

5

THE morning after the fight at the saloon, Zeb Coulson bought a special edition of the Carver *Star*. Tom poured himself some freshly-brewed coffee and settled down to read what Judd had written.

The story of what had happened at the saloon was told beneath the headline *NEW MARSHAL WAGES WAR ON LAWLESS ELEMENT!* Carver's 'new constable,' it said, had revealed 'his phenomenal skill with pistol and fist by defeating not one but two rowdy patrons of the Oriental Sunset in a single-handed display of skill and fair play.' Tom, remembering the way Bill Tanner's dead body had looked propped up against the bar, dismissed the remainder of the report immediately.

"How you feelin' today, Tom?" the

youngster enquired cautiously.

Tom's smile was faint. "Hungry."

"I'll go fetch some food in a while. How's Daggett?"

Tom told him. This morning, as was his custom, Tom had woken early and gone out back to wash and shave. He'd looked in on Daggett only to find him sitting on the edge of his mattress, a look of fear and anger on his ugly face. From the dark rings beneath his eyes, Tom could see he hadn't slept much.

The freighter had been surly, gruffly warning Tom of the consequences of not releasing him. Tom had laughed without humour and disappeared from view.

Later, when Zeb returned from the diner, Tom kicked a tray of food through the gap at the bottom of the cell door and left Daggett to it. It was up to him whether or not he ate the food provided for him. As it turned out, he did.

A short time later, Tom began his

first patrol of the day. Today was the day Jason Birchell was due to return to Carver, the day he would discover that his foreman had been arrested by the new town marshal. The day he would discover just who that town marshal was.

Although he was deep in thought, his grey-blue eyes automatically shifted back and forth across the busy street, and what drew his attention now was a man standing on the corner of the opposite boardwalk, staring at him.

The man presented no immediate threat, but there was something in the way he stood, weight resting on his left leg, hands at his sides, just staring, that warned Tom to watch him.

He was tall, like Tom himself, and wore high-heeled boots beneath faded levis. Over his cotton shirt he wore a leather waistcoat, and around his spare hips hung a well-tended gunbelt. Even from this distance, Tom saw the keen light of intelligence in the man's dark eyes.

"Marshal?"

Tom turned to look down at a plump woman in her middle-fifties. Her large bosom was like a shelf stretching out across her chest, and her dress was buttoned right up to the neck despite the heat that was growing with every minute.

"Ma'am?" he enquired politely.

"It's about the report in this morning's *Star*," she said.

"Yes'm?"

"Could I ask you something?"

"Surely, ma'am."

Tom threw a glance over his shoulder at the corner of the opposite boardwalk. He heard the woman asking him if he intended to enforce the law with his gun all the time, and if he did, would it be safe for people like herself to walk the streets? It took a while for him to form an answer, because his mind was elsewhere.

The man in the leather vest had vanished.

Hunter's roan whickered softly when he stepped into the livery stable. A quick look assured him that his horse was being well cared for. Behind him, a tall, thin man in his mid-thirties with a clean set of regular features topped by a mane of thick brown hair, stepped forward. He wore a pair of stained coveralls and carried a curry-comb he'd just been cleaning. His name, Tom had discovered, was Keegan, and he worked here for Greaves, the stable-owner.

"Howdy, marshal."

Tom nodded a greeting and indicated his horse. "I see you're doing a good job," he said.

"Wouldn't know how to do a bad 'un."

Tom went into the stall with his horse, speaking softly as he unhooked his saddle-blanket from the wall at the far end and threw it across the animal's broad back. As he saddled up, working with practised ease, he made idle conversation with the stable-man. Shortly, the horse was being led out towards the stable doors. It was then that Tom turned and studied Keegan shrewdly.

"Have you seen a man around town today wearing a cotton shirt and a leather vest?" he asked on impulse. "He's tall and dark, and carries a pistol like he knows what it's there for."

Keegan thought for a moment. "Yep," he replied. "I seen him, all right. That's his cayuse yonder." He pointed to a stall at the rear of the stable, in which a black and white mustang stood. It was a small animal, but its lines were graceful. "Don't know his name or where he's stayin', but he come to town 'bout three days ago."

About the same time as me, Tom thought. Aloud, he said, "Thanks, Keegan. Just wondered." He led the roan out into the sunlight.

This morning he'd decided to go for a ride, and told Zeb to watch the shop for a couple of hours. It would be a useful exercise to familiarise himself with the surrounding countryside and, in any case, a horse like the roan was never happier than when being given free rein across the open plains.

He climbed up into the saddle, clucked the horse into motion and left Carver behind him.

A ride was just what he and the horse needed; the roan because the gallop came naturally to him, and Tom because the diversion would relax and prepare him for his coming confrontation with Birchell.

As much as he enjoyed town life and the community spirit, there was no substitute for the open prairie, with its clusters of red-tipped Apache plumes waving gently to and fro among the endless sea of sage, manzanita and saguarro. He had been away from it all for too long, and had determined never again to take any of it for granted.

When he was far enough from town, he dismounted and tied one rein around his saddlehorn, allowing the other to hang down from the bit. That way the roan could graze contentedly, but if it should start to wander, it would eventually trip on the loose rein and come to a halt.

Afoot now, Tom scanned the land around him. He was in a draw which led into a small canyon. His keen eyes spotted nothing out of the ordinary. After satisfying himself that he was alone, he turned, so that the sun was behind him, and tried a couple of practice pulls, lifting his Colt, aiming but never firing.

He shifted his balance, flexed his fingers, then drew again and again. He didn't want it to come to shooting when he saw Birchell again, but if it did, he wanted to be in good shape. He'd waited too long for this moment just to end up dying in the dirt with a bullet in his guts.

He checked the action of the Colt, making sure it was in good working order and free from dust. Out here, the heat could play hell with a man's gun. He reholstered the weapon, then drew again, fast. This time he cocked, aimed and fired. The shot echoed across the draw, and the top of a bunch of Apache plumes thirty feet away burst apart.

He repeated the exercise until his ammunition — five rounds, with the hammer always set down over the empty sixth chamber — was spent. Then he decided to call it a day.

It was in that moment, when he was halfway through re-loading — and thus at his most vulnerable — that he realised he was being watched.

He froze for a moment, fighting the urge to look around. He didn't know for sure yet that someone *was* out there; it was just instinct, a vague, inexplicable itching in his shoulder-blades.

Carefully, deliberately, he finished reloading, holstered the Colt and turned, slowly, to face the roan. In that pivot he took in the surrounding brush. A few oddly-shaped cacti, some clumps of mesquite, a few boulders — plenty of cover for someone to hide in. So where *was* he?

He?

For all Tom knew, there could be more than one of them.

With long strides he closed the distance between him and the horse. Mounting up, he noticed how the animal's ears had pricked up. Bending forward, he peered between them in order to find the direction from which the disturbance had come. According to that, the watcher — or *watchers* — were in a patch of rocks and weeds about eighty yards to the north.

A Mexican badger scuttled by, and he nearly drew his gun. Forcing himself to relax a little, he let his breath out in a cold hiss, then clucked the horse into a canter. He rode back-straight, ready to dig his heels into the roan's flanks and ride hell-for-leather the minute he heard the rolling report of a rifle or the high-pitched whine of a handgun.

But he heard nothing.

He relaxed a little more, confident he was now out of long-gun range. Whoever had been spying on him, he decided, had obviously been there to do just that — spy. The opportunity to kill him from ambush had presented itself a dozen or more times during the ride, and yet nothing had happened. Which made it all the more curious.

There was something going on in Carver. But what? As marshal, it was his job to find out.

When he got back to town, he led the roan into the stable and handed the reins to Keegan. Under normal circumstances he would have seen to the horse himself, but right now he was anxious to get across the street and under cover someplace, so he could wait and see if whoever had spied on him returned to town.

"See to him for me, will you, Keegan? I — " He stopped suddenly, then barked, "Where's that mustang?"

Keegan followed his gaze to the empty stall at the rear of the stable, in which the small mustang belonging to the mysterious newcomer in the leather vest had been kept. Keegan said, "That feller, the one we was speakin' about? He came in, asked me to saddle up for him. He went ridin'."

"When?"

"Musta been ten minutes, a quarter-hour after you." It was obvious from his tone that the stable-hand failed to see the significance — or the connection — of his words.

Tom let out a long breath. "Thanks."

Later, heading for his office, he tried to consider all the angles. It certainly looked as if the drifter had followed him.

But *why*?

When Clem Beecher poked his head around the office door, Tom, who had been flicking through some out-of-date wanted notices, looked up quickly. Seeing the mayor, he relaxed and tried to paste on a smile.

He had been in a quiet mood, waiting for Birchell to get back to town, hear the news and come storming across to demand Ike Daggett's release.

The clock on the wall said three-fifty. Daggett had told him Birchell would be getting back to town sometime during the late afternoon. The time was getting close.

"Supper, tonight, around seven," Beecher told him briefly.

Fleetingly the new marshal wondered what his situation would be come seven tonight. "Uh," he replied awkwardly, fishing for an excuse. "I don't know. I guess I should really stay here — "

"You've only got to stay for supper," the mayor pointed out. "Not the whole evening."

"All right," Tom replied with a smile.

Beecher paused, halfway between the open door and the jamb. They were alone in the office, Zeb having gone on patrol ten minutes earlier. Beecher asked, "Everything all right, son? You seem a mite . . . preoccupied."

"I'm fine. Just . . . "

"What?"

"Nothing. Tired, I guess. I didn't

124

sleep much last night," he lied.

Remembering last night's outbreak of violence, Beecher nodded his understanding. "I should've thought," he said. "Look, if you really *don't* want to come over tonight . . . "

"I do," Tom told him. "I will."

That was when they heard footsteps on the boardwalk outside, and a voice said, "Good afternoon, Mr Beecher. Excuse me, would you?"

Tom felt his skin tingle as all the memories and hatred started to rise within him. Beecher moved away from the door to allow a second man to pass through into the office, and Tom felt his throat tighten imperceptibly.

At last, he found himself face to face with Jason Birchell.

He was dressed in a well-tailored grey suit, with a brocade vest and black string tie over a crisp white shirt. He was still a heavy man who had about him an air of big business and wealth, and his face was hard and tanned beneath hair the colour of gunmetal.

"You'll be Mr Birchell," Tom said quietly.

"I am," Birchell replied, adding perfunctorily, "Pleased to meet you, marshal. Congratulations on your appointment; well-deserved. I'm sure." He hardly looked at Tom; not that it would have made much difference if he had. Six years was a long time, — and Tom had done a lot of growing up in Yuma. "I'm here to sort out this misunderstanding you had with Ike Daggett."

Beecher glanced from one man to the other, sensing the tension that had come into the new lawman. "There was no misunderstanding, Mr Birchell," he explained equably. "Your men tried to — "

"It's all right, Clem," Tom cut in, keeping his eyes on Birchell. "I'll see to this."

Beecher glanced at him, still puzzled by the vague sense of ill-feeling in the room. Still, Tom had a point, he

126

guessed. He *was* the marshal. It was up to him to handle this business with Daggett without outside interference. "All right," he said slowly. "Guess I'll be moving along, then."

Tom nodded. "See you tonight."

When the door closed behind him, Birchell licked his lips. Tom watched him very closely. He couldn't see a handgun, but that didn't mean a thing. Birchell could be wearing a shoulder-rig beneath his expensive suit, or carrying a concealed over-and-under.

"Take a seat?" Tom asked casually.

"I'll stand, thanks all the same," Birchell replied.

Tom shrugged. He hadn't been sure how he'd react when he finally set eyes on Birchell again. He still wasn't sure how he felt.

"About Ike," Birchell said briskly. "I — "

"Forget Ike," Tom replied. He came around the desk, closed the distance fast and threw a satisfying roundhouse right that sent Birchell

127

stumbling backwards.

The older, heavier man made a sound of surprise just before he slammed into the door, bounced off and fell to his knees. The next time he looked up, a line of blood bisected his chin, and still more of it stained his yellowing teeth. "What . . . what . . . "

Tom glared down at him, breathing hard. "I've waited six years to do that," he gritted.

Birchell ran a hand across his glistening face. His skin was crimson with fury. "I don't know what you're — "

Tom lashed out again, grabbing his right-side lapel. He hauled Birchell back to his feet and slapped him hard. For just an instant Birchell's dark eyes burned bright, and his right hand turned into a claw above a non-existent sidearm. Then he recovered himself. "Just what in hell do you think you're playin' at? Who *are* you?"

Tom met his gaze, and the intensity of his stare forbade Birchell to glance away. "You mean to say you *really* don't know?" he asked.

Birchell's breathing calmed down a little then. His eyes narrowed to slits as he looked directly into the starpacker's face.

Finally, after throwing a glance sideways to make sure the cell-block door was shut and that they wouldn't be overheard, he husked, "It *is* you, isn't it?" He wiped some more blood from his chin. "Christ . . . I thought you were dead."

Tom crossed back to the desk and rested his weight on its edge. "No," he replied. "But they made me pay for your crime. They gave me ten years in the Yuma Pen. I served just over half of 'em before they gave me parole."

Tom had to give him his due. For all Birchell knew, Tom was planning to put a bullet in his guts right here and now, but when the shock wore off, it was curiosity, not fear, that took over. "So," Birchell asked. "What is it, then? You traced me here, found out I'd invested my money, thought you could blackmail me?"

Tom shook his head. "No," he said again. "Because what I want can't be bought with money." He saw the look on Birchell's face and laughed icily. "Oh, don't fret. I'm not going to kill you. I wanted to, at first. When I realised you'd set me up. I guess I killed you a hundred times here, in my head. But not any more."

"*What* then?" Birchell demanded, dabbing at his chin. He didn't show any fear at all now, just annoyance, as if he wanted to get whatever foolishness Tom had planned over and done with, then get on with his life.

Tom looked at him hard for a moment before saying, "You're going to confess, Birchell."

"*What?*"

"You're going to write everything down — how you pulled the job, where you buried the bullion, how you disposed of it and how you got me drunk that night and set me up."

Much to Tom's chagrin, Birchell

laughed heartily. "You're crazy!"

"No," Tom replied flatly.

Birchell held his gaze with his own pig-like eyes. "Then you must be stupid," he said.

Tom came up off the desk and struck out again, feeling the force of the blow all the way up to his shoulder.

The heavier man loosed an oath as he spilled back a step, dropping his kerchief. Tom reached out and again grabbed him by the lapels. He swung Birchell around and slammed him up against the gun-rack, causing him to groan and reach around to hold his punished back.

"You *are* crazy!" Birchell rasped.

Tom shook his head, advancing on the other man like some relentless, unstoppable angel of vengeance.

"You *must* be!" Birchell panted. "Who else but a madman would think up such a half-baked notion?" he asked. "Well? What good will a confession do to you? Huh? Have you really stopped to think about it?"

Tom faltered, unnerved by his quarry's apparent confidence.

"Things have changed, Hunter," Birchell said contemptuously. "I've come a long way in the last six years. Gained influence and respect." He wiped his bloody nose on his cuff. "All right — where's your quill and ink? I'll write your damn' confession for you, and be glad to do it! But I'll tell you here an' now, it won't be worth a whore's promise by the time my lawyers get through with telling the court how it was obtained!"

Tom's jaw muscles worked at a furious rate. He felt anger, confusion and injustice, because as much as he hated to acknowledge the fact, Birchell was right. He *hadn't* thought it through. He'd just assumed that a signed confession would settle everything.

"What about your money?" he asked suddenly. "As far as folks hereabouts know, you made that rounding up cattle and selling 'em in the mining towns just after the War. Happen that was true, you'd have receipts, bills of sale."

"Hell, that would've been twenty years ago!"

"Maybe," Tom agreed. "But those mining towns had gone without beef for years during the War. First few herds to come through would've caused quite a stir, I imagine. Maybe you'll give me the names of those towns, and I'll check 'em out."

But Birchell only laughed again. "You're clutching at straws now, Hunter!" he spat. "Face it — a confession'll get you nowhere. It'll be your word against mine. And who's gonna believe *you*?" He shook his head. "The only way you'll ever get even with me is by using *that*." He pointed to Tom's Colt, then held his arms out, making a target of himself. "Well?" he said defiantly. "I'm waiting. Go on — kill me if you've a mind to."

Tom's left cheek twitched, but he made no move to draw the weapon.

"Go on," Birchell insisted. "A bullet

right here should do it." He patted the straining belly beneath his brocade vest. "That's what you'd really like, isn't it? To see me die slow, in agony?"

Tom said and did nothing, causing Birchell to regard him with disgust. "If you haven't got the guts for it, then," he hissed, "get, the hell out of my way. I've got business elsewhere."

He brushed past the stunned lawman and headed for the door. Tom turned and watched him go, by turns hating the man more than ever and reluctantly admiring his undoubted courage.

"Birchell," he called at last. The other man swung around, still dabbing at his bloody face. "This won't end here," he promised quietly.

Birchell snorted. "Dream on, you sorry sonofabitch," he said disdainfully. "Our business ended six years ago — only you were too dumb to realise it."

Then he tore open the door and slammed it viciously behind him.

After his confrontation with Birchell, Tom just wanted to go someplace alone and consider his next move. As much as he valued their friendship, the last thing he needed was supper with the Beechers. Still, he was committed now.

Once he'd calmed down enough to replay the encounter through his mind, he began to realise that, on the surface at least, little had changed. Tom doubted that Birchell would reveal his past to anyone else. To do that might draw unwelcome attention to his own erstwhile career.

For the time being, then, the starpacker's reputation was safe.

Still, he hadn't been prepared for Birchell's reaction to their meeting, and it had rattled him bad. In his mind he'd seen the former road-agent turn pale at the sight of him; watched his resolve crumble; witnessed his signature on a written confession and finally experienced the long-denied satisfaction of having his name cleared.

But now . . .

Now he began to see things from Birchell's perspective.

That he would have to tread wary from this moment forward he had no doubt. Unless he misjudged Birchell completely, the sonofabuck would already be making moves to have him killed. As long as he was alive, Tom was a threat. And Birchell, with his wealth and social standing, would not tolerate *that*.

Tread wary, then. And try to come up with another way to get even with the man, short of stepping outside the law and shooting him dead.

Somehow Tom made it through the evening without betraying his distraction. Over mutton stew he smiled and conversed politely with the mayor and his wife, then made his excuses and quit the dry-goods store to set off at a slow pace back to the law office.

The streets had quietened down now, cooled off too and, overhead, the sky was an unreachable purple shroud across which had been scattered a thousand diamonds. Tom tipped his hat to a couple of passing townsfolk, and paused to exchange a few pleasanties with Smallwood, the storekeeper.

Wagon and horseback traffic had grown sparse. Up ahead, the town lamplighter was busy illuminating Front Street. Carver had about it an air of tranquillity but, try as he might, Tom could not make himself relax long enough to enjoy it.

He continued on his way up the street, stopping occasionally to check that all the stores were locked up tight. And it was whilst he was thus engaged that he began to feel that familiar itch starting up between his shoulder-blades again.

Turning quickly, he saw the mystery-man in the leather vest watching him from across the street. For just a moment their eyes met across the gloomy distance, but Tom found the other man's weathered face unreadable.

There was no doubt that he'd been watching the lawman. Following him too, most likely.

Without stopping to think about it, Tom stepped to the edge of the boardwalk. It was high time he braced the other man. But Leather Vest, guessing his intention, quickly turned and started off along his side of the street.

Tom made to step off the boardwalk, but was unable to pursue him straight-away. At that moment, a four-strong team of draught horses appeared, hauling a prairie schooner along the dusty stem. The marshal waited impatiently for it to pass. As it did so, rattling and creaking on straining springs, he read the legend painted on its dusty canvas cover: BIRCHELL FREIGHT CO.

Then the wagon was gone.

As was Leather Vest.

Tom drew deeply of the cool night air as he scanned the other side of the street.

Empty.

"Damn!"

He paused there for one moment longer, listening to moths tapping desperately at the streetlamps above. Then he turned and continued on towards the office.

6

THE following day Tom made it a point to locate, and attempt to question, the vest-wearing stranger. Unless he was mistaken, the situation with Birchell had turned into a waiting game, with each man hanging fire until the other made a move, so he guessed he might as well use the time wisely.

The first couple of hotels he tried, including the one he himself had booked into upon his arrival in town, yielded little. So did the two boarding-houses Zeb suggested he try. But at the Mason House on Carlyle Street, a man answering Leather Vest's description had booked in four days earlier under the name of Bob Cole.

The name meant nothing to Tom. Maybe it was an alias. He asked if 'Mr Cole' was in his room. He wasn't. In that case, he told the clerk, he wanted to see the fellow's quarters.

"Is he a bad man, this fellow Cole?" the clerk asked worriedly. "I wouldn't want any trouble here, marshal."

He took a key from the rack on the wall and led Tom upstairs to the first floor. He let them into a square, clean room with sunlight trapped in a blinding white splash on the linoleum, and watched curiously as the marshal went through saddle-bags and dresser-drawers.

"Find anythin'?" the clerk enquired.

Tom shook his head.

Back at the law office he began to go through the stacks of wanted dodgers his predecessor had allowed to accumulate. There was just a chance that Cole's name or likeness might have been posted at some time or another. As it turned out, however, Tom found no trace of him.

Later that afternoon, Hobart, the bank manager, sent a cashier over to ask if he would sit in on a meeting

141

with some visiting head-office officials. Evidently Hobart wanted him to say something reassuring about the security at the Carver branch.

The meeting dragged on for a while, as one item followed another, but once he'd said his piece, Tom allowed his thoughts to turn back to Birchell. A whole day had passed since they'd locked horns in his office. What plans had he made, or set into motion, to deal with Tom?

At around five o'clock. Tom quit the bank and combined a patrol of town with a trip to the diner across the street. Although he kept his eyes peeled for any sign of Bob Cole, he failed to sight the man anywhere. Neither did he see anything of Birchell.

The evening passed uneventfully, save for one minor altercation down at the Dancing Lady. Once that was settled Tom took a final, cautious turn around town and, upon returning to the office, sent Zeb on home.

No sooner had he closed the door

behind the youngster than Ike Daggett called out, "Hey, starpacker!"

Tom threw his hat onto the desk and gave a sigh. He was in no mood for Daggett, but he supposed he ought to go see what the freighter had found to complain about this time. He went through to the cell-block and was again struck by the man's uncanny resemblance to a wild animal. Leaning on the doorframe he asked, "What's the matter?"

Daggett came up off his bunk and gripped the bars of his cell so tight that his knuckles showed white in the oil-lamp's flickering yellow glow. "We alone at last, lawman?"

Tom nodded.

"Good. "Cause what I got to say, I don't think you'd want too many other people to hear."

At once Tom felt an uneasy stirring in the pit of his stomach. He knew what was coming without any shadow of doubt, but held his silence.

"See that door you're restin' up

against, marshal?" Daggett remarked. "Made of mighty thin wood, I'd say. So thin that a body can hear right through it."

The lawman forced himself to sound unconcerned. "Is that a fact?"

"So thin," the freighter went on, obviously enjoying himself, "that I didn't have no trouble at all hearin' ever'thin' you an' Jase Birchell said out there yest'day afternoon." He giggled. "Didn't say anythin' 'bout it right away, o' course. Figured you might have other things on your mind. But I'm tellin' you *now*."

"You're all heart, Daggett."

The freighter's smile died. "I don't think you understand me, marshal. I heard *all* of it. And I figure you might 'preciate my silence. Can't hardly think the town council'd hire an ex-con to keep the peace, so I reckon you musta kept pretty quiet about it when you 'plied for the job." He dribbled into his beard. "Am I right?" he asked eagerly.

"So what's the deal?" Tom asked tiredly, although he could guess what was coming.

"Unlock the goddam door," Daggett snarled. "Let me out of here. Say . . . say I saw the error o' my ways." He laughed shortly. "Yeah, that'll do it. Let me outta here an' I won't breathe a word. Keep me behind bars an' I'll sing just like the kind of bird you *do* keep in a cage."

"And who do you suppose'll listen?" Tom asked, trying a bluff. "Tell whoever you damn' well like, Daggett. But remember something. You tell part of the story and you'll have to tell *all* of it. Can't hardly imagine Birchell'd cotton much to that."

Daggett moved back from the bars, nodding slowly as if assuring himself that he understood the position. Even so, he asked, "That your final word, lawdog?"

In reply, Tom straightened up, turned and started back into the main office. He took one step before he heard the triple click of a gun being cocked. Daggett snarled, "That's far enough! Turn 'round an' keep your hands up. That's it. Now come back here."

It was an old but well-kept Walker Colt. In Daggett's big paws it looked more like a child's toy, but Tom recognised the real thing when he saw it, and knew that if he didn't obey, he'd be sharing his guts with a .44 calibre slug.

He moved slowly back into the cell-block, keeping his hands shoulder-high.

"That's better," Daggett said. "Well done, marshal. First smart thing I seen you do yet."

"Where'd you get that gun?" Tom asked in a low voice. He already knew the answer, of course, and spoke it aloud. "Someone dropped it through the window, right?" He indicated the window at the top of the far wall, where someone in the yard beyond could have reached up, passed it through, maybe wrapped in a flour sack to protect it when it hit the floor. He said, "Was it Birchell? He put you up to this?"

"Get those keys out'n your pocket, starpacker," Daggett replied, enjoying his new-found power. "That's right, reach across with your left hand. Good."

"You're a fool, Daggett. What will you do now? You can't stay in Carver. At most, the circuit judge would've given you a fine. Like this, you're only making things worse."

"Shut up," Daggett ordered. "Gimme those keys." He reached his own left hand through the bars and snatched the key-ring from Tom's fingers.

"Birchell put you up to this, didn't he," Tom said as a statement. "What did he tell you? That he'd pay you to kill me?" He saw by the look in Daggett's eyes that he had struck the truth, or something very close to it. "If you accept his word for anything, you're a fool, Daggett. He let me take the blame for a double killing and robbery he committed six years ago . . . " He let his voice trail off. It would do no good to keep on talking. Daggett was pushing the cell door open, breathing deeply as if the air should taste somehow different now.

"I don't give a damn what Birchell did in the past," the freighter growled. "He's footin' the bill right now, an' that's all that matters. I've killed men before, marshal. I know how to do it, an' I ain't afeared to do it. You'll be just one more." He was half-in, half-out of the cell.

Tom licked his lips. He had under-estimated Birchell. Again. He certainly hadn't expected the man to come up with a trick like this. An ambush, a well-staged 'accident,' sure; but not this.

Still, he wasn't just going to stand around waiting for it to happen. Daggett was going to kill him, nothing surer, so he had nothing to lose. *Nothing*.

He moved quickly, hoping to crowd the big freighter before he could fire the Colt. He didn't try for his own weapon, still holstered. That would have taken too much time, as fast as he was. Instead he moved forward, grabbed one of the bars on the cell door and slammed it shut.

It was a heavy door and it swung in on well-oiled hinges. Daggett yelled out in a mixture of surprise and pain. Instinctively he tried to get out from between the door and the frame, struggling to twist the gun so that it still pointed at Tom, who had thrown his weight against the cell door. Again he grunted in pain through clenched, rotting teeth as Tom quickly pulled the door open and slammed it shut again, this time trapping Daggett's right wrist. The freighter opened his fingers involuntarily and the Colt thudded to the floor.

Wrenching the door open again, Tom grabbed the bigger man by his stained buckskin shirt and threw him back so that he hit the wall hard. He moved in, knowing full well that all he had to do to finish it was take a step back and relock the door.

But that would have been the easy way, locking Daggett back in and boarding up the window so that Birchell couldn't try the same trick again. And right then, the easy way held no appeal for him. Tom had waited six years to get even with Birchell. Now he figured he'd just about taken enough.

Daggett saw him coming and cowered as Tom came within striking distance. Then, quick for a man of his size and weight, he struck out with a left jab. He exhibited an almost graceful way of moving as the punch landed and sent Tom back a pace, his right cheek numb.

"Come on then, you little bastard!" Daggett rasped. "I can just as easy kill you with my bare hands!" And he lunged forward, eager, arms outstretched.

Here in the confines of the cell there wasn't much room to manoeuvre. Daggett came in quickly, grinning evilly through his shaggy beard. His arms went around Tom and tightened without mercy in a bear-hug. Tom's own arms were trapped at his sides. His feet left the plank floorboards as Daggett lifted him like a child. Daggett's triumphant laugh and Tom's breathless groan were the only sounds in the room.

A rushing sound filled the lawman's ears. He found himself unable to breath. Screwing his eyes tight shut, he tried to force Daggett's thick arms open, to ease the pressure on his ribs, but couldn't. The rushing sound grew louder until it became a roar. He opened his eyes and felt a jerk of panic when all he could see before them was a misty red curtain.

Then, somehow, he managed to summon enough strength to bend his left leg and straighten it savagely, so that the pointed toe of his boot bit hard into Daggett's shin. Over the sound of rushing blood he heard Daggett grunt an oath. Tom lifted his left leg, the right one too, and straightened them both at the same time. Daggett's arms opened just a little, enough for Tom to suck greedily at the warm air of the cell-block. He kicked again; again; again; and then he was pushing Daggett's arms wider and wider and the rushing in his ears was growing softer.

All at once he fell out of Daggett's grip and staggered back to come up sharp against the bars of the cell. His face was pale and sweaty, his expression carved in lines of anger. He took a step toward Daggett and the big man knew that this was it the final, do-or-die clash.

But then a voice barked, "*Hold it!*"

The sound of the Walker Colt being

cocked came to his ears for the second time that evening, and Tom froze, swallowed and turned slowly around.

Birchell stood in the cell-block doorway, the Colt aimed at his stomach. He was wearing a grey check suit and a burgundy-coloured cravat. He was smiling, but it was a cold smile, laced with disgust.

Behind him stood two men. Tom recognised them as Daggett's drinking-partners. One had a flowing moustache, a couple of scars showing through his deep tan. The other was bearded, shorter than the first but still above six feet. Both were thickset and unkempt. They were hard men, to whom the lives of others meant little or nothing. They waited in silence as Birchell said to Daggett, "Take his gun."

Daggett limped forward a pace and yanked Tom's Colt from leather. By the time he stepped back the weapon was cocked and aimed. Tom stared at Birchell as if he were the only man in the room; as if he wasn't aiming a handgun at him; as if he didn't have the upper hand.

"What now?" he asked softly.

Birchell showed his teeth in a grin. "What now?" he repeated. "If I had my way, I'd put one of these bullets into your brain and get you out of my hair once and for all, but a gunshot would attract too much attention. Don't worry, though *marshal*. I've got something planned that'll be just as effective."

Tom couldn't guess what Birchell had in mind for him, but whatever it was was unlikely to be very pleasant.

"I'll want his ears, Taylor," Birchell told the man with the moustache. "That way I'll know you've done a thorough job."

"Don't worry, Mr Birchell," Taylor replied. "For the kind of bonus you've got waitin' for us, there won't be no mistakes."

"Right," Birchell told him. He turned to Tom. "Be seein' you, Hunter." He smiled coldly. "Put him out, Ike."

Daggett uncocked the gun, slipped it into the waistband of his pants and stepped forward, that eager, sadistic look back on his face. He pushed Tom roughly out of the cell and followed close behind, towering over the badge-toter like some fairy-tale giant.

Birchell said, "And listen, Ike. When it's done, I want you back in here behind those bars."

"Aw . . . "

"That way," Birchell went on persuasively, "they won't connect you with Hunter's sudden disappearance. Don't worry, I'll pay your fine when the circuit judge turns up."

Daggett was silent for a moment. Then he said, "All right, boss." They watched Birchell turn and saunter out of the office and into the night.

Tom wondered if that would be the last time he'd ever see Birchell. He hoped not, because if there *was* a next time, he'd just kill the bastard and have done with it.

Further thought was cut short, however, as Daggett bunched a fist the size of a pineapple and punched him deep in the guts. Tom doubled up, feeling the pain of his already-bruised ribs about to make him black out. Daggett's clenched fists struck him hard against the base of the neck and he saw stars as he went down onto his knees. A hard, savage kick lifted him up and then left him breathless.

He was bruised; sore; *unconscious*.

Della Vine, the saloon-girl who had been struck by the late Bill Tanner in the Oriental Sunset a few nights before, stood on the deserted porch outside the saloon, getting some fresh air.

The mark on her left cheek was camouflaged by powder and rouge, but ever since that night, when her shrill scream had brought the marshal to full awareness and triggered the gunshot that filled the drinking-parlour with thunder, she had been under the weather.

She felt tired. It seemed like she'd been around forever. She'd whored in a dozen towns like this one, making a living at about the only thing in life she did passably well. But maybe now it was time to quit.

Occasionally she paused to reflect on her misspent life, but at this stage of the game there was little real point. She would never know the joy of watching her children grow up, or feel a husband's comforting arm encircle her waist. There would be no cosying down before a roaring fire while winter snows piled up outside, so why waste time pondering over it?

These disillusioned thoughts were running through her head as she stood alone on the porch outside the saloon. The night had grown chilly as she leaned against the hitch-rack, half listening to a familiar honky-tonk melody coming from the Pianola inside. She was looking down-town when she saw a man come out of the marshal's office.

Of course, there was nothing unusual in that. But gradually a frown began to wrinkle her powdered brow. For few men were Ike Daggett's height and build, and Ike Daggett, she had thought, was in jail.

So what was he now doing out in the street?

She moved back into the shadow cast by the porch overhang, one hand to her mouth, the other in a tense ball at her flat stomach. She watched curiously as three more figures came out of the office, two of them men much like Daggett and the third, although tall and well-proportioned, obviously smaller in comparison.

She let out a small whimper as she recognised the marshal. Judging from the way Daggett's two companions were dragging him, the lawman must be unconscious — maybe even dead.

Her stomach began to flutter when she realised that she was the only witness to what was happening.

Although Daggett was striding toward

her on the opposite side of the street, it soon became obvious that she was invisible there in the shadows. Daggett turned right without seeing her, down a side alley, and the other two dragged the unconscious marshal along behind him.

At once she felt the agony of indecision. What should she do? Go tell the marshal's young deputy? The mayor, perhaps? Quickly she decided to tell her boss, and let him take it from there. Yes, that was it.

She turned and started toward the batwings, where yellow light spilled out into a puddle on the weathered boardwalk. Before she could reach them, however, she felt two masculine arms come around her from behind, one trapping her thin arms against her sides, the other clasping her mouth shut and stifling her scream.

When her assailant spoke, his breath was hot and rasping in her ear. "Now just you hold on a second . . ."

For a long, long time there was nothing but darkness. Darkness and silence.

Then, slowly, the darkness began to turn grey as Tom surfaced from oblivion.

He had no idea where he was or how long he'd been there. At first he couldn't even remember the events which had led to this moment. Then, suddenly, everything came back to him with startling clarity.

His head ached. His heart pounded. His fight with Daggett and the subsequent beating had left him exhausted. But he was as determined as ever not to go down without a struggle.

Warily he glanced around. He was lying on his side in a shallow, moon-silvered bowl of land surrounded by brush and cactus. A paloverde tree rose up from the centre of the clearing to scratch at the night sky. About thirty feet away, four horses had been ground-hitched. Three of them were saddled. The fourth, which the starpacker assumed he'd been thrown across for the ride out to this lonely spot, was bare save for an old Indian blanket.

Hunkered close to the horses were three men, Daggett, Taylor and the shorter, bearded freighter whose name he had not yet heard spoken. They were talking in undertones.

As Tom tried to sit up they turned to face him. Their expressions were impossible to read in the poor, flickering light of the small fire they'd lit to ward off the desert chill.

Without a word, Daggett rose to his full height and stamped over. He, too, seemed to scrape at the starry sky as he loomed over the lawman. In the background, Daggett's companions watched with fire-reddened faces as they passed a bottle of jig-juice back and forth between them.

"You ready to die, starpacker?" Daggett asked softly.

Tom had been feeling his teeth with his tongue. Now he worked up some saliva and spat into the underbrush. "Are *you*?" he replied.

Daggett reached down and pulled him to his feet. The freighter and his partners had been so sure they had Tom where they wanted him that they hadn't even bothered to tie him. But such carelessness might be to his advantage.

Keeping his eyes on those of the lawman, Daggett called over his shoulder, "Peters — fetch the rope.

The skin on Tom's face tightened as the third man rose and trotted over to the horses. He unhooked a coil of hemp from his saddlehorn and carried it into the centre of the clearing.

He tossed one end up into the shadowy branches above. It came down on the other side of the sturdiest limb. As Tom swallowed softly, the man began to busy himself fashioning a crude but serviceable noose.

"'Cordin' to what Birchell said," Daggett muttered through the cool, anticipatory smile that stretched his lips, "you should'a hung years back, starpacker."

"For a crime I didn't commit?" Tom asked in disgust.

Daggett shrugged. The rights and wrongs of the business didn't concern him so long as he got paid. He put one hand on Tom's left shoulder and pushed him over to the tree, saying, "Taylor — get mounted."

"*Yo!*"

Tom struggled to keep his breathing at a steady rate, forcing himself to wait for an opening he might be able to exploit. The cool night air had gone a long way to reviving him, and fear of the noose had sharpened his mind.

Peters was still tying the noose. Taylor was cutting his horse from the small bunch. The only one not otherwise engaged was Daggett.

One out of three, then.

Tom didn't think he was likely to get better odds any time soon.

With a defiant roar he slammed his elbow back into Daggett's paunch and the bigger man yelped in surprise. As he buckled at the waist and clutched at his injured stomach, Tom wheeled to the left and began to race for the surrounding tangle of mesquite and brittlebush. If he could just make it to some cover he might be able to disappear into the darkness.

Behind him all three of the freighters began yelling in confusion. He heard a gunblast but forced his legs to keep pumping. Before he could reach the edge of the clearing, which still lay about ten feet away, however, someone — Peters, he thought — barrelled into him and smashed him to the ground.

The breath flew out of him in a rush. He caught his forehead against the rock-littered ground. Someone rolled him over and a fist awoke fresh pain his jaw.

After that he knew he didn't stand a chance. All three of them were upon him in a confused kaleidoscope of faces and fists. He was rolled back onto his stomach and his hands were tied roughly behind him. Then he was hauled back to his feet and dragged over to the waiting noose.

"You wily little bastard," Daggett spat angrily. He dropped the noose over Tom's head and tightened the slip-knot so that the rough hemp dug into the soft muscle around his neck. Then he directed Taylor to take the other end of the rope, wind it around his saddlehorn, mount up and await his command to move.

The only sounds in the clearing now were the crackling of the small fire and Tom's laboured breathing.

Daggett stepped away from him and said, "All right, Taylor — *do* it."

Taylor kicked his heels into the flanks of his dun gelding and the animal began to walk steadily off into the darkness. With infinite slowness the rope began to draw taut, then pull the Carver lawman inexorably up onto his tiptoes and beyond . . .

Tom's sweat-slick face twisted into a grimace. His teeth ground together as he fought to snap the bonds holding his wrists. Taylor urged his horse still further into the shadows and Tom's boots left the ground altogether.

"*Aghhhh . . .*"

His growl was a constricted, phlegmy sound, and it mixed anger and frustration in equal measures. The lawman's kicking feet lifted one more painful inch from the ground and the noose grew tighter still, slowly tearing flesh.

"*Uhhh . . .*"

Daggett's eyes fairly glowed as he watched the execution. Tom kicked his legs some more, swayed back and forth, began to twist lazily so that he could see the faces of all three of his killers.

Then —

A gunblast shattered the moment, and Taylor screamed and flung up his arms as a thick streak of blood leapt from his chest to splash his horse's mane. He back-flipped from the terrified mount, and now that he was no longer holding it, the rope wound around his saddlehorn quickly unravelled, dropping Tom back to the ground.

As the marshal collapsed in a heap, he heard the mechanical *click-click* of someone levering a shell into the breech of a Winchester, and then, "All right, pilgrims. Get your hands high. Both of you!"

The voice came from out of the shadows to the south. It was a cold voice, quiet but commanding. Daggett, trying to identify it and also playing for time, said. "Don't shoot no more, mister! You . . . you a road-agent or somethin'?"

"Nope," replied his unseen attacker. "Now get your damn' hands up, like I said."

Daggett swore, but seeing no other option, started to raise his hands. They only got as high as his waist, however; then he grabbed Tom's Colt and hauled it from where it had been tucked inside his belt.

Crouching to make himself a smaller target, he thumbed back the hammer and fired lethal orange flame into the night. Even before the shot had died away, he was leaping for the cover of the undergrowth on the other side of the clearing.

Within seconds he and Peters, who had gone for his Dance Brothers Army .44, had set up a barrage of return fire, peppering the darkness with lead in the hopes of plugging the concealed rifleman.

The horses stamped and whinnied. A wild bullet, ploughing into the small fire, exploded embers everywhere. On the ground beneath the tree, Tom tried to suck at the air and escape the ropes binding his hands behind his back.

Meanwhile, his hidden saviour was proving to be an able marksman. Before Peters could empty his .44, he shrugged, spun, yelled something unintelligible and hit the sand with a hole in his throat.

After that the gunfire ceased abruptly.

Daggett had disappeared into the brush to the north, so there was nobody left to shoot at. Tom heard the faraway sounds the big man made crashing through the foliage and tried again to snap his bonds.

Then he heard footsteps behind him and he froze. A shadow fell across him, then melted into the ground as the man who cast it hunkered down beside him and gently loosened the noose at his neck.

Cool, fresh air had never tasted so good. While Tom gulped at it greedily, the newcomer took out a Texas Bowie knife and cut the rope from his wrists. Then the man turned him carefully onto his back and helped him sit up against the bole of the tree.

And Tom came face to face with Bob Cole — the mysterious stranger in the leather vest.

7

"*YOU!*" Tom croaked.

"Yeah, me," said the stranger. "Now shut up."

Propping his rifle up against the tree beside Tom, he slipped the knife into the sheath on the left side of his weapons belt and went across to inspect the two bodies. A moment later he turned back to the lawman and stared down at him with surprising concern.

"Feel all right?" he asked.

Tom swallowed and nodded, fingering the lacerated skin around his neck. "Sure. Thanks to you."

The stranger was about Tom's own age, possibly a couple of years older. His hair was as dark as his eyes, and cut short beneath a wide-brimmed black hat. He was clean-shaven and moderately handsome, and his sidearm,

Tom noticed, was a pretty business-like Smith & Wesson American. "We'll head on back to town in a while," the fellow said. "Once you've got your breath back."

"Daggett — "

"Forget about Daggett. We'll catch up with him sooner or later."

Tom cleared his throat again. Talking was still an effort, but there were things that had to be said. "Don't think I'm ungrateful, Cole, but . . . you mind telling me just who you are, and why you bought into this?"

The stranger smiled. "Well," he said, "for a start, my name isn't Cole. Cole's just an alias. My real name is Philip Denning. I'm a U.S. marshal." He reached into his shirt pocket and brought out a wallet, which he opened to reveal his shield of office.

"*What?*"

"You heard," Denning replied. "Look, just give me a minute to go fetch my horse, then I'll explain everything."

Denning turned and trotted off into

the brush. About three-quarters of a minute later he reappeared, leading his mustang. He put his Winchester back in its sheath and hobbled the animal with those belonging to the freighters.

Finally he hunkered down beside Tom and took out a Durham sack. As he built himself a quirley he said, "Well — had any ideas what this is all about yet?"

Tom had a shrewd notion, but didn't want to tip his hand straightaway. "Maybe," he replied cautiously. "You've obviously been dogging me for a reason. Tell me what it is and I'll see if I was right."

Denning cracked an easy smile. "Fair enough," he said, nodding. When their eyes, met, he said two words, very clearly. "The bullion."

Tom frowned. "The bullion from the stagecoach hold-up?"

"Yep." Denning confirmed. "As you know, it was never recovered. The authorities dug up half of Arizona looking for it, but they never found it."

"That's because Birchell — "

"I know, I know. I read all the trial reports, Hunter. I know what your defence was. Chances are I know more about you than you do yourself."

"So that's why they paroled me early, is it?" Tom mused, piecing everything together as he spoke. "In the hopes that I'd lead you straight to it."

Denning shrugged. "Something like that," he agreed. "Only it didn't go exactly to plan. You drifted for a while, and picked up a job with Charlie Goodnight. Instead of heading straight for the bullion, you worked up a stake and came here — by way of that run-down little spread thirty miles back."

"You saw what happened there?"

"Saw it all."

"That old woman," Tom said quietly. "She was the stagecoach driver's widow."

"I guessed as much."

"And you've been following me all these months?"

"Right from the first day you left

Yuma," Denning said, obviously proud of the fact that he'd been able to maintain his anonymity as long as he had. "Got to admit, I wasn't sure *what* you were planning when you finally reached Carver. Gave me quite a surprise when they made you marshal. Thought at first you'd just come gunning for the man you claimed'd set you up."

"The man who *did* set me up."

Denning held up a placating palm. "All right, all right, don't get your bowels in an uproar! I believe you, Hunter. Had my doubts at first, but seeing how things've panned out . . . "

"Does that mean you can get the case reopened?" Tom asked eagerly.

"Not hardly. I don't believe I've got that much clout. But it *does* mean you've got someone in your corner at last. And two heads're better than one when it comes to thinking up ways to trap rats like Birchell." He stubbed out what remained of his cigarette and rose to his feet. "Anyway, that's enough gab for one night, I think. Rest up a while, starpacker. I'll get these here bodies strapped across their saddles and we'll take 'em back to town with us."

Tom nodded. "Here, I'll give you a hand . . ."

"Save it; I'll manage."

Tom drew deeply at the air. "You know," he said soberly, "I must be luckier than I thought. If you hadn't been riding in my shadow, those fellers would've killed me tonight, and given Birchell my ears as a keepsake."

"You're luckier than you know," Denning replied as he set to work at his ghoulish task. "If it hadn't been for a little lady by the name of Della Vine, I wouldn't even known you'd left town."

"Huh?"

Denning forced a laugh to cover his revulsion at handling the bodies. "It was her who saw Daggett and his friends carrying you out of the law office and down an alleyway. I'd just come back from answering a call of nature when

175

I caught sight of her heading back into the saloon. I figured she looked kind of anxious about something, and played a hunch by stopping her to find out what it was."

When Tom made no comment, the federal lawman frowned down at him. "Hunter? You all right?"

Tom came out of his reverie. "Uh, sure. Just thinking." He was silent for a while longer, until he reached a decision. "I think it's about time I told the mayor everything," he said. "He's been good to me, and I owe him the truth." His smile was rueful. "I'm not going to relish the telling of it," he confessed. "But at least now I've got a U.S. marshal to back me up."

The other man considered the wisdom of Tom's decision before commenting. "Can he keep a secret, this mayor?" he asked.

"I reckon."

"Good. Because I'd as soon certain parts of what happened tonight didn't become common knowledge just yet.

We'll let Birchell simmer for a while, and with any luck he'll end up spooking so bad he'll make a fatal mistake."

Ike Daggett swallowed two fingers of whiskey and held his tumbler out for a refill. Jason Birchell sat across the desk from him, nursing a tumbler of his own. Reaching forward, he raised a bottle and splashed more whiskey into Daggett's glass. The big freighter drank it down greedily, spilling some of the amber liquid down his beard. Disgusted, Birchell stood up and began to pace the carpet, his impatience obvious.

They were in Birchell's office. Midnight was still a quarter-hour away. The shades had been drawn and the only illumination came from a kerosene lamp on the writing-bureau in the corner.

After a while Birchell asked, "You're *sure* you've got no idea who this bushwhacker was?" His voice was harsh and demanding, and the words issued from tight, angry lips.

"No idea, boss. I couldn't recognise the voice or nothin'. But . . . "

"What?" Birchell demanded eagerly.

"But we know it weren't Hunter's kid deputy." Daggett finished lamely.

Birchell cursed beneath his breath. "I didn't ask you who you thought it *wasn't*," he rasped. He sat down at his desk again, lacing his fingers together. A moment later he asked, "How badly did you hurt Hunter? Do you think he was almost dead?"

Daggett swallowed some more whiskey. Gradually he stopped trembling, although his lips remained dry and his eyes were wide and red-rimmed. "I don't know. We beat him up pretty good, an' he spent a fair spell kickin' in the air." He considered. "He's gotta be in pretty bad shape, boss; he's *gotta* be."

"But not at death's door," Birchell said.

"I guess not," Daggett agreed quietly.

"Well, at least the other two won't

sing," the freight boss remarked with a sigh. "That's something, I suppose. They can't pin anything on me. *Yet*." His eyes suddenly bored into Daggett. "It's a different story for you, though, Ike."

Daggett jumped, visibly startled. He stared with glassy eyes as Birchell went on. "If you'd done the job properly, we could've locked you back in your cell and no-one would've been any the wiser. They'd never have connected you with the marshal's disappearance." Birchell made an arch of his fingers, resting his forehead on it and closing his eyes. When he spoke, his voice was like winter. "You better get out of town, Ike."

Daggett frowned, slowly taking in the menacing of the words. "But . . . but I got no money, no cayuse. I — "

"Get the hell out of town," Birchell said through clenched teeth. "Get out — or I'll kill you."

Silence entered the office then, a thick, cloying silence upon which the

179

threat hung heavily. Daggett got to his feet, slowly rising to his full height. His dark eyes burned into Birchell's, but when he spoke there was desperation in his tone, and it was pathetic.

"You're makin' a big mistake, boss, you know that? I could go straight to the mayor right now an' tell him ever'thin', if'n I had a mind to. And if Hunter *does* pull through, well, between us, we could put you away for a long time. Maybe even get you hung."

Birchell pursed his fleshy lips. Daggett was right, of course. He *did* pose a threat. But only for as long as he lived. Birchell had no reservations about taking his Colt from the top right-hand drawer and putting a bullet between the freighter's eyes. Still, there might yet be a way to avoid such an unsociable act.

"Come on, Ike. Let's not kid one another. You know as well as I do that if you sing we'll *both* go down, an' you don't want to die or rot in prison any more than I do. Just get out of town while the gettin's good. Quit the territory. Here, I'll even give you a grubstake."

He opened the drawer and reached inside. Daggett watched through eyes narrowed with suspicion. They widened when Birchell brought his revolver up, pointing the barrel at Daggett's chest, dead centre.

"Sit down," he ordered.

Daggett stood transfixed, looking into the round barrel. "You wouldn't — " he began, but then his voice trailed off, because he knew that Birchell *would*. He sat down again, slowly.

"That's better," said Birchell, all business again. "Now, relax. Maybe I was being a mite hasty." He'd made his point and gained Daggett's fear. He aimed the gun away from the big man and leaned forward conspiratorially. "We've got to work together on this one, Ike, because we're *both* involved now. Understand?"

Their eyes met. Nothing in the office

moved except the clock on the mantel, ticking away to midnight. After a while, Daggett said softly, "What do you want me to do?"

Birchell said, "Run a message for me. Not tonight, maybe not tomorrow. Maybe never. I'll have to find out just how badly we've hurt Hunter first. If he's still alive this time tomorrow night, I'll want you to contact someone who can solve all our problems for us."

Daggett frowned. "Who?"

But Birchell was too busy muttering to himself to reply. "I wonder who that bushwhacker was? Maybe just a drifter, maybe something more. No matter." His sigh was heavy. "Ike — you can hole up in the cellar beneath the loading-bay out back. It's dry enough in there and you can have a lamp. I'll get you some food and a canteen of water. You should be safe enough."

"Who can get us out of this if Hunter pulls through?" Daggett demanded impatiently.

"Lee Knight," Birchell told him, and

there was a triumphant gleam in his eyes as he spoke the name.

Daggett's face went slack. "You mean — ?"

Birchell nodded, cutting him short. "Yeah," he replied. "Lee Knight. The most dangerous gunman in the whole damn' southwest."

By the time Tom and Denning rode back into town, leading the death-horses behind them, it was well past midnight, so there was no-one around to watch their slow passage along Front Street.

Three-quarters of the way along the main thoroughfare they reined in before Beecher's store, and while Denning tied the animals to the hitch-rack outside, Tom went up onto the boardwalk, around to the side entrance to Beecher's home, cleared his throat and rapped softly on the door.

It took six or seven minutes before a light showed in the darkness beyond the curtains. By then Denning had joined him in the empty alleyway. The mayor appeared beyond the portal, holding a lamp. He asked who was there and Tom told him.

Once he and the U.S. marshal had been allowed inside, things grew a bit confused. In the yellow lamplight Tom's beaten and bruised condition was easy to see. A thin, crusty ring of dried blood encircled his neck, and two dark smudges looped his eyes.

Beecher's expression betrayed his shock. "What in — ! Great heavens! What happened? Emmy, we've got to clean this boy up! Put some water on to boil; coffee, too!"

"Wait," Tom said tiredly. The single word made the mayor and his wife pause in their efforts to usher him through to the parlour. They stared at him with curiosity plain on their sleep-puffed faces. "I've got something to tell you first," he said. "Once you've heard it, you can decide if you still want to help me."

"What? Tom, boy — "

"Hear him out," said Denning.

They did.

Afterwards, Beecher ran one hand through his iron-grey hair and shook his head. According to the grandfather clock standing beside the parlour door, the time was one-fifteen. "Is all this true?" the mayor asked Denning. The federal lawman nodded. "And you came all this way just to try and clear your name?" said Beecher, addressing Tom. "All this way — after all these years?"

Tom didn't meet his gaze. "Uh-huh."

"Judas, boy . . . " Beecher's eyes grew distant and glazed. "This . . . this is just incredible!" He stood up and took a turn around the cluttered room. "I'll be honest with you," he said at length. "Had you told me all this the first time we met, I wouldn't have let you within a mile of that badge on your chest, although Lord knows, you wouldn't be the first owlhoot to set yourself up as a peacekeeper."

"That's about what I thought," Tom confessed quietly.

"But now . . . " Beecher shook his head some more. "Hell, boy . . . " He sighed. "A while ago, you told us that once we'd heard you out we could decide whether or not we still wanted to help you, right?"

"Yessir."

The mayor nodded. "All right," he said briskly. "Get that water boilin', Emmy. Looks to me like our town marshal needs a little fixin' up!"

The news broke soon enough next morning. Ike Daggett, foreman of the town's freighting company, had escaped from jail. Two of his friends had tried to help him break out, but there had been a running fight and they had been shot dead, as far as was known, by the marshal alone. Daggett had managed to get away, but not before inflicting several minor wounds on the new starpacker.

This was the story Ed Judd received

from Clem Beecher, and it was these facts he was busy writing into a lead article in the back room of the *Star*'s office when Jason Birchell came in.

As part-owner of the *Star*, Birchell was a frequent visitor, and having a newspaper in his pocket had distinct advantages at times like this. "Howdy, Ed. How's things?"

Judd, a square-faced, balding man with a deep, gentle voice arid blue eyes, glanced up from his copy. "Uh . . . hello, Jase. Take a seat. I was planning to drop in on you later today."

"Oh? Why's that?"

"Haven't you heard about this business with Ike Daggett?"

Keeping his expression carefully neutral, Birchell said. "Oh, sure. Hell, that's why I came *here*. You know what it's like out on the street. Nobody really knows anything about what happened last night, but they're all ready to throw in their ten cents' worth. Just what *did* happen?"

Briefly Judd repeated what Beecher had told him, and Birchell allowed himself a sigh of relief when he heard it, for it seemed that he was in the clear, thank God.

But why had the mayor come out with such a misleading version of the truth? What was he hoping to gain? Then again, however, maybe Beecher was only repeating what Hunter had chosen to tell *him*.

"How is the marshal?" he asked curiously. "He all right?"

Judd took out a pipe and stuck it between his teeth. He blew through it a couple of times, then began to pack the bowl with Union Leader cut plug. "He's fine," he said. "Scratched up some, the way I hear it, but otherwise okay."

Daggett would have to run that message to Lee Knight, then, Birchell decided. He said, "What was it you wanted from me?"

"Oh, just a few comments on Ike Daggett."

188

"Such as?"

"Well," said the editor, striking a match, "why do you suppose he busted out of jail? He wasn't arrested for anything drastic. A couple of weeks in the pokey, maybe a fine, and it would've all been forgotten. Now . . . "

Birchell suddenly saw a good chance to spread some mud as far as Hunter was concerned. Every little helped, he told himself as he assumed a pained expression and said, "I've been wondering about that myself, Ed. I know Ike was a rough-and-tumble kind of feller, but he had nothing against spending a couple of weeks behind bars, taking things easy and getting three squares a day inside him. I can't help thinking . . . "

Judd, a born journalist, sat forward, sensing a possible story. "What?" he asked bluntly.

Birchell played his hand for all it was worth. "It's nothing — I guess," he said, feigning discomfort.

"Come on now, Jase. It's my job to

view all the angles. Let's hear it."

Birchell's sigh was heavy. "Well," he lied smoothly, "as I said, Ike didn't have anything against spending a couple of weeks in the calaboose, so I can't think why he decided to bust out. Unless . . . " He paused for good measure, then looked Judd straight in the eye. He had the newspaperman caught like a fish on a hook. "I guess you know that the marshal threatened Ike almost the minute he rode into town?"

"No, I didn't know that."

"Yeah. Couple fellers work for me were drinking with Ike over at the Sunset when all of a sudden the marshal tried to pick a fight with him for no good reason. You can ask Josh Casey, the bartender at the Sunset. He saw the whole thing. So did a couple o' my boys." Casey and Birchell's freighters would witness anything for a healthy bonus at the end of the week, but he left that unsaid.

Judd asked, "What are you trying to say, then, Jase? Come on, man, out with it."

Birchell wore such a look of sincerity that it never occurred to Judd to doubt him when he said softly, "The marshal had it in for Ike right from the start. I don't know why, but that's how it seems to me." He leaned even closer to say, "I don't know how he did it, Ed, but he must've made Ike so damn' desperate he just *had* to bust out last night."

Judd stayed stock-still for what seemed like a long time. His pipe hung from between his lips like a horse-thief from a cottonwood. He said, "Well . . . that's an angle I sure never figured. Think perhaps I'll take a look into it."

Birchell nodded, his business almost done. "Well, remember Ed, I'm only voicing an opinion."

"But if there're witnesses . . . "

"Oh, there's witnesses all right," Birchell confirmed. "See what you can dig up, then. Might sell a couple extra copies of the *Star* if nothing else." He got to his feet.

"One last thing, Jase," Judd said.

"Sure."

"Where do you think Ike is right now?"

Birchell joined his eyebrows in thought. "Well, if I know Ike, he's about halfway to New Mexico by now."

"He wouldn't have come back to town, then?"

"No," Birchell said, moving to the door. "He'll be long gone by now. You can rely on it."

Young Zeb, being just a boy, saw only excitement in the previous night's jailbreak, but since Tom had told him much the same story as Beecher had told Judd, the straw-haired youngster could hardly be blamed for failing to appreciate the affair's wider implications.

Tom made his first call of the day to the town gunsmith's store. When he came back to the law office, a new Frontier Colt sat in the holster of his buscadero weapons belt. He had spent a good forty minutes testing the handgun on the firing-range out back of the store, and after the arms dealer had made one or two minor modifications, the Colt felt comfortable in his palm.

Tom himself, however, looked pale and drained. Beecher who'd been shooting the breeze with Zeb, noticed it the minute he closed the door behind him and hung his hat on a peg in the wall, but refrained from making any comment until Zeb left the office to patrol town.

"You all right, Tom?" he asked gently. "You're lookin' a mite peaked."

Tom poured himself a mug of stewed coffee and shook his head. "I'm fine. Just tired is all."

"You *should* be," Beecher replied. "But it's more than that, isn't it? You're not sure Denning's right." He was referring to part of the advice the

U.S. marshal had given them during the early hours. "You don't *want* to wait for Birchell to make a wrong move, do you? You want to go on over to his office and settle it one way or the other right *now*."

Tom smiled wearily. "Is it that obvious?" he asked. "Hell, I don't know. I came here with the intention of nailing Birchell *legally*. I'd still prefer to do it that way if I could. But maybe that stagecoach-robbing sonofabitch was right when he told me the only way I'd ever get even with him was by using my gun."

Beecher came over to him. "That's a point," he said, setting one hip on the desk. "What *is* it about that gun? There's nothing special about it that I can see, and yet you've been eyeing it and touching it ever since you came in."

There was an unmistakable aura of sorrow in Tom when he looked into Beecher's face. He appeared old and used, and the hell of it was that he wasn't even thirty yet. He said, "That's because I think I'm going to have to use it again," and there was a calm acceptance in his voice that was frightening. "Soon."

8

LEE KNIGHT loved guns.

In the grey-green gloom of his hotel room, with the tattered curtains closed against the harsh glare of the day's sun, he lay back on his bed, legs crossed at the ankles, and thought about little else. He imagined hauling back hammers and squeezing triggers, levering shells into Winchesters and cocking, then firing Spencers. He recalled the sharp, acrid stench of cordite in his nostrils and the momentary loss of hearing that always came after the roar of a gunshot, and to him it was how taking a virgin or drinking a gallon of snake-head might be to other men.

But as much as Knight loved guns, he loved killing even more. That was where the *real* thrill lay. As much as he loved the New Line Police Colts held firmly in his hands, they could never hope to beat the joy of the kill for him. Never.

Lee Knight was of average height and slight build. The fair hair that fringed his high forehead was ringed with tight curls. His beard was trimmed close to his chin, and framed a long, thin face with a sharp, aquiline nose and dark-brown eyes. If a man can truly be both young and old at the same time, then that's what Knight was; ageless. It was difficult, in fact, to remember a time when he *hadn't* been around.

Knight wasn't his real name, of course, but he'd adopted it so many years before that few people could still recall the original. He'd taken the name about eighteen months after he'd killed his first man. Eighteen months after he'd discovered his abnormal love of death and the weapons that could so swiftly bring it.

Not that he wore black. Unlike many of his counterparts, Knight's wardrobe was almost disarming; a plain butternut shirt and creased denim pants, with a matching, waist-length jacket. Over the back of a chair in one corner hung a plain, brown leather gunbelt with cutaway holsters and rawhide thongs, and his low-crowned planter's hat sat on the chest of drawers beside the bed.

At first he didn't hear the tapping at the door. He was too busy trying to remember all the times he'd used his .38s and watched men die while he lived on triumphant. He was thinking about Le Mats, Colts, Smith and Wessons, Merwin and Hulberts, Remingtons, Starrs and Tranters, and he knew that before long, just like always, he would bring to mind all the rifles, the Winchesters, Sharps', Henrys, Hawkens and Spencers.

Then the tapping came again and he frowned like a spoilt child whose playthings are suddenly taken away from him. Casually he aimed his Colts at the panels of the door and said, "Who's there?"

The answer came back muffled. "Name's Daggett. I got a job for you, if you're int'rested."

"Come in slowly," Knight called back. "And if you're wearing a gun, you'd better keep your hands away from it."

The door opened gradually and Daggett appeared in the frame, bent forward slightly with his eyes narrowed to pierce the gloom after the light of the hallway outside. After a moment he saw the man on the bed with the guns pointed at him, and instinctively his arms came up, well away from his sides.

He'd spent a day cooped up in the cellar beneath Birchell's loading-bay, drinking brackish water and chewing stale biscuits and cold beans in the meagre light of a lantern that soon made the trapped air stink of kerosene, and in his gut had been a fluttery feeling that he might be discovered at any moment.

But nothing untoward had occurred,

nothing until Birchell had pulled the trap-door and called him out at two-thirty in the morning.

Overhead, the sky had been as black as pitch. As he'd stretched his cramped muscles, Birchell had told him, "Hunter's all right. Fit as a flea, the way Ed Judd tells it."

"That's crazy! I — "

"Let's not argue about it, Ike! Hunter's still a threat to us, that's the main thing."

Daggett fell silent, like a chastised guard dog. "You'll be wantin' me to run a message to this Knight *hombre*, then," he'd said at last.

"Yeah. Here." Birchell gave him a letter. "You'll find Knight in Pedregal."

Daggett nodded. He knew the copper-mining town, which lay about four days' hard ride to the north and west.

Birchell led him to a waiting pinto, explaining that all the provisions he was likely to need had been packed into the saddle-bags. Daggett mounted up awkwardly, unused to horseback riding. Before long he'd quit town and disappeared into the darkness.

He rode like hell all through what remained of the night, and the following noon found a patch of scrubby shade beneath which to sit out the worst of the day's heat. At around five in the afternoon, he was back in the saddle.

And now, four days later, here he was.

Pedregal.

He'd ridden into town late the night before, but had decided against finding Knight straight away. Instead he'd gone to an all-night bath-house and washed the grit out of his pores.

He slept in the same stall he'd rented for the pinto. Then, first thing this morning, he'd started his search for the gunman. And now he'd found him — in a dingy little room on the third floor of a rooming-house that had rats in the backyard and roaches crawling up the walls.

"You're Knight," he said at last.

"And you're Daggett," Knight replied. "Now we know each other, what's the job?"

Daggett felt his temper slipping. He didn't much care for the gunman's attitude, but there wasn't a whole lot he could do about it. "You, ah, you mind pointin' them guns someplace else?" he asked cautiously.

"Sure," said Knight. "You were saying?"

When the Colts were pointed at the ceiling he felt a little more like talking. He put his arms down and very carefully pulled the envelope Birchell had given him from his pocket and handed it to Knight. As the gunman unfolded and scanned the message, Daggett explained, "It's a letter of introduction."

"That much I can see for myself," Knight replied sarcastically. He tossed the letter aside. "All right. I know Birchell from way back. He says you've got all the details. So . . . talk."

Daggett said, "There's a man in

Carver, the town marshal. He's become a problem to Birchell. You know what lawmen're like. The boss thought you c'd . . . handle 'im."

"What do you mean, 'handle' him?" Knight asked, sitting forward with a creak of bedsprings. "You mean *kill* him?"

Daggett paused, not fully comprehending the point Knight was trying to make. "I . . . yeah," he muttered.

"Well say so," Knight spat in disgust. "I wish to Christ people would say what they mean."

There was an uncomfortable silence in the gloomy little room. Then Dagget asked softly, "Can you do it?"

"For a thousand bucks I can."

The freighter released a sigh. Birchell had given him a figure he couldn't go beyond. If Knight had asked for any more than a thousand dollars, he would have had to find some way of telling the gunman he was too expensive.

"Then . . . I guess it's settled," he mumbled.

"Yep," Knight replied. "I guess it is at that."

They left Pedregal that same afternoon.

It was a vast land, flat as a pancake and dry, and as they rode, the sun above squeezed tiny droplets of sweat from their skin and caked them with the sketchy pallor of salt. It was a God-forsaken land, and Dagget had had a bellyfull of it during the past few days, but Knight rode back-straight in the centre-fire rig on his muscular bay gelding and made no complaint. Daggett, meanwhile, cursed, sighed and grumbled until it was too hot even for that.

They made camp at a muddy water-hole when the sun was at its hottest, and sat out the heat in the questionable shade of some Joshua trees. Then they were up again, tightening cinches and climbing into saddles, clucking their horses forward and moving on across the desert country.

According to what Knight had said back at his hotel room, he and Birchell went back a way together. Daggett, his dark eyes red-rimmed by the sand that a rare desert breeze had blown into them, wondered what the two men had in common. He'd heard rumours among the other freighters that Birchell had been pretty handy with a gun in years gone by, and Daggett believed it. But had the fat man ever been in Knight's league?

Having felt Birchell's wrath in the past, it was, he guessed, quite possible.

That night they came across an old Indian settlement that had been abandoned sixty or more years earlier. Daggett had seen the place on his way to Pedregal. It was a small cluster of adobe huts. He had ridden well clear of it, reluctant to camp there alone for the night.

But maybe things would be better with someone there to keep him company, although fine company Knight was, speaking only rarely, and then just to issue a command or pass some sarcastic remark.

A shiver ran the length of his spine as they entered the ghost-town. Maybe it was just the night chill, maybe something in the way the wind sent little dust-devils spiralling down the narrow alleyways. Pack-rats ran back and forth, their tiny claws tapping, and for a moment, Daggett — not usually given to imagination — thought of all the stories he'd ever heard about phantom drummers still beating tattoos on forgotten battlegrounds . . .

When Knight came up behind him, as soundless as a wraith, he jumped. "You just gonna stand around?" the gunman enquired. "Or are you gonna help me make camp?"

Daggett said weakly, "I'll . . . what do you want me to do?"

"Take the horses into the flat-roofed hut over yonder, the one with part of the doorway missing. There's feed for 'em in the sack behind my left-side saddle-bag." Knight handed him the reins to his bay along with those of the freighter's wiry little pinto. "I'll make a fire, cook up some coffee."

Hesitantly, Daggett led the animals into the darkness of the old hut, stumbling occasionally on pieces of fallen masonry. Overhead, night had descended with inky blackness, and the wind, finding broken walls to blow through, howled like a Navajo shaman.

He off-saddled the animals, ground-hobbled and watered them, then scattered feed across the floor before walking with jerky, nervous steps across to the *jacal* Knight had claimed as their own.

The fire the gunman had built lit the interior with amber shadows, and Daggett saw that it had once been decent living-quarters for some long-dead family. Though it was badly decayed now, however, the hardy adobe walls would help keep out some of the biting wind.

Knight had made coffee and set a

can of tomatoes to boil in a pot over the flames. Knight himself sat cross-legged, watching the steam rise from the mug he held in both his hands. Daggett reached across to pour himself a cup, then caught the brief flash of warning in the gunman's brown eyes. He said, "Ah . . . all right if I, ah, he'p myself?"

He felt anger flaring inside him as he heard himself speak the words. Ike Daggett, the big, bad freighter, asking for a cup of coffee like a snot-nosed kid! As much as he hated to admit it, though, Knight scared him stiff.

"Go ahead," Knight offered.

Daggett poured himself the coffee, then sat back to watch the dancing flames. Knight didn't look into the fire at all. Daggett said, "Tomatoes sure smell good."

"Yep," Knight agreed. "Let 'em boil a while longer and they'll be just right."

Daggett drained his mug. More for something to say than anything else, he mumbled, "I've heard of you, Knight. Off an' on. Birchell says you're 'bout the most dangerous man in the whole southwest."

"Does he now?"

"Uh-huh. Me, I heard all 'bout the men you've killed. All of 'em in face-to-face shoot-outs, too, never any bushwhackin' or back-shootin'. Seems . . . you got quite a rep."

The conversation died before it really had a chance to get started. A branch in the fire snapped and sent sparks high into the air, where they burned out like dying stars. Then, after stirring the tomatoes once, Knight asked, "Why does Birchell want this lawman's clock stopped?"

Daggett said, "Far as I know, him an' Birchell go 'way back together, an' the marshal's got somethin' on Birchell that could bring him big grief if it ever got out."

"Any idea what?"

"Nope," Daggett lied. "All I know is it was important enough to Birchell for him to send me to fetch you."

When Knight turned his eyes onto Daggett, the freighter realised he could no longer feel any heat coming from the fire. The sensation persisted as Knight studied him closely. Then the gunman put his mug down, straightened his legs out and sat back against one of the plain, pocked walls. His eyes narrowed shrewdly. "Aw, come on," he urged. "You know what it's about, all right." He leaned forward again, and his voice dropped to just a whisper. "Tell me, Daggett. What is it that makes this lawman worth a thousand bucks dead?" Again he said, "Tell me," but this time it was an order, not a request.

"I don't know nothin' I ain't already told you," Daggett complained. He felt the heat of the fire again now, only this time it seemed hotter than before.

"You know, all right," Knight stated flatly. When he smiled he reminded Daggett of Apache squaws hovering over helpless, wounded soldiers after a skirmish. "Why, I feel downright *certain* you know more'n you're letting on. In fact — " and here he got to his knees and peeked into the pot to check on its contents, "I reckon you know enough to've made your *own* play at blackmailing Birchell."

"*What?*" Daggett said. "That's a lie!"

But he'd said it too quickly, and he knew it.

"Then why else would Birchell want *you* dead, too?" Knight enquired.

The gunman's comment, voiced with genuine curiosity, didn't register at first, until Daggett realised exactly what he'd said. "M — me?"

Knight was smiling, but this was no joke. Outside, the wind sent dust flying everywhere. Pack-rats squealed. The horses stomped their hooves and whinnied. Knight said, "Didn't it occur to you to wonder why Birchell didn't just wire me 'stead of sending you all this way to fetch me?"

He reached into his jacket pocket and pulled out a folded sheet. He handed it to Daggett. "Here, take a look," he invited. "You *can* read, can't you?"

Like a fool, Daggett nodded, taking the sheet with clumsy fingers. When he unfolded it he saw Western Union's trademark. He read the message printed beneath it twice, with lips that moved soundlessly.

L KNIGHT, PEDREGAL, ARIZ TERR.
JOB FOR YOU HERE STOP MESSENGER ARRIVING WITH DETAILS FOUR DAYS FROM THIS DATE STOP MESSENGER PLUS JOB HERE $1500.00 FOR BOTH STOP WIRE WITH CONFIRMATION SIGNED BIRCHELL.

Knight said, "You understand it? It means — "

"*I know what it means!*" Daggett snapped.

"It means," Knight continued patiently, "that I'm charging Birchell a thousand

212

bucks for the lawman, and only five hundred for you." He frowned suddenly. "Now why don't you tell me why he wants you out of the way?"

"Ain't it obvious?" Daggett replied, breathing hard. "He don't want nobody left around who knows the whole story!"

"And what *is* the whole story?"

"God-*damn*, Knight! You gotta give me a break!" Desperate now, Daggett went on in a flood of words. "He'll settle with you, too! Just wait and see. he'll get rid of you soon as you've done his dirty work for him. Then there won't be *anyone* left who can touch him!" He leaned forward, face contorted beneath the bushy black shadow of his beard. "Years ago, he did a bullion job, killed a couple of fellers. He framed the marshal, let him take the blame for it. Marshal was only a kid then, but Birchell still set 'im up and let 'im go to the Yuma Pen! That's the kinda man he is!"

Knight gave an expressive sigh, as

if he were considering the situation. Then he said, "He's the kind who's hiring me. That's all I know."

"Come *on*, Knight! Give me a — " Abruptly, the words stopped. Daggett knew there'd be no mercy from the other man, just death.

Knight pulled his right-side Colt from its holster, and against his will, Daggett flinched and cried out. Knight, however, only smiled. "Get up," he said sharply. "Come on, come on. Outside."

Both men got to their feet, Knight easily, Daggett slowly. The freighter towered above the gunman like a grizzly bear, but with the gun in his fist, Knight wasn't small at all. He jerked the weapon a couple of times toward the doorway. "Move," he said impatiently.

Daggett crouched as he went out into the night. A strong wind whipped his hair across his forehead and he narrowed his eyes against the flying dust. Although he didn't wear a gun, he figured he had two advantages over his would-be assassin; he was bigger, and he was heavier. If he could just get Knight in a bear-hug, the gunman wouldn't be able to do a damn' thing about it except wait for his ribs to cave in and then die.

He turned to face the other man, who stood watching him with a strange brightness in his eyes, and sized up the distance between them. Could Knight cock and fire his pistol before Daggett reached out, grabbed him and started to squeeze the life out of him? Just how fast could a man be, for God's sake?

Around them the wind continued to howl like a Cheyenne death-song. It moaned, steadily rising in volume, then faded away, only to rise again.

Daggett shuddered. "Gimme a break, will you?" he implored.

Knight just shook his head. His lips formed the word very carefully before he said it. "No."

That was it, then. It was now or never. With a roar of defiance, the freighter threw himself at the gunman, his long, thick arms outstretched. A sudden gust of wind tugged at his buckskins, slowing him down; even so, he was just about to grab Knight when Knight cocked the .38 with the edge of his left hand and fired.

"For the love'a God, man — !"

He fired again and again, the expression on his face never changing.

Daggett took a step back, as if pushed by invisible hands. By the time the second and third bullets struck him, he was stumbling like a drunk. Two more shots blew the night apart. Then Daggett fell to his knees with five holes in his chest and five crimson streamers leaking out of them. His face was dead white against the blackness of his beard as all two hundred and sixty pounds of him hit the dirt face-first.

Knight knew without having to check that he was finished. The kicking of his legs was just delayed reaction.

The wind howled again, brushing against the gunman's flushed face and wafting the smell of gunsmoke to his nostrils. It gave an edge to his appetite. Reloading the .38 in a series of quick, economical movements, he went back into the adobe hut, where he fished the steaming tomatoes out of the pot and onto a plate and ate them with great relish.

By next morning, the wind had blown sand up around Daggett's still form. Tonight, when the wind returned, it would cover him with still more. By the time Knight reached Carver, it would have buried him completely.

Provided the pack-rats didn't get to him first.

With a copy of the Carver *Star* held out at arm's length, the old woman with the piercing black eyes and the wrinkled, tanned skin squinted, focusing on the headline that said *NEW MARSHAL WAGES WAR ON LAWLESS ELEMENT!* Briefly, picking out a passage here and there, she read the account for what must have been the tenth time, and then threw the paper onto the smooth, well-scrubbed table, her long, hooked fingers knitting together in obvious agitation. She shook her grey head and muttered something scornful beneath her breath.

Coming up behind her, her daughter Bonnie knelt down and put an arm around her. When she spoke, her voice was miserable and sad. "Ma . . . ma, you got to forget about that." She indicated the newspaper report.

Her mother was quiet for a long time; so long, in fact, that when she finally *did* speak, the sound of her voice made the girl jump. "I can't forget about him as murdered yore pa, child," she said. "Imagine, him comin' straight outta prison an' gettin' hisself a respons'ble job like marshal o' Carver! Shouldn't be allowed! Why, I bet them there town council fellers don't even *know* 'bout his wicked ways — though they soon will iffen he keeps up with *these* tricks!"

The young girl sighed. It was no

good. Ever since those two drifters had passed through three days earlier and given them a couple of dollars and a copy of the *Star* in return for a cup of coffee and a small cooked meal, the old woman had been like this. She liked to read, although her eyesight was failing, and often passed the time with a few treasured books, but as soon as she'd started reading the front page of the newspaper . . .

"Says here he killed some feller in a gunfight," the old woman told her daughter, seemingly unaware that Bonnie had already read the account for herself. "Says the feller was raisin' Ned." She laughed grimly. "I bet he was just lettin' off a little steam, enjoyin' hisself." Her bottom lip quivered dangerously until she regained control of herself. "Well," she remarked. "Didn't take Hunter long to slip back into old habits."

"But ma — "

"But nothin', child." And the old woman would say no more.

But at dawn the following morning, Bonnie came out onto the sagging porch to see her mother in front of the house with their thick-bodied old nag between the traces of their sagging buckboard. The old woman was throwing a bag into the back of the light wagon as the girl came down off the porch.

"Ma?"

The old woman turned and fixed her daughter with a hard stare. "Don't try an' stop me," she rasped. "I've thought about it an' I've thought about it. I can't sleep nights for thinkin' as how the man who killed my poor John is wearin' a badge an' killin' more folks right on my doorstep. Someone's gotta tell them town council fellers just what's what 'bout their lawman, an' it might's well be me."

"But ma — "

"I said not to try an stop me, didn't I?" The old woman's stern tone held the girl frozen. After a moment, the fire in her eyes cooled. "That's better."

With a groan she hauled her aged frame up into the seat and took the reins in her gnarled hands. "Look after the place while I'm gone, child. I'll be back directly."

"But ma . . . " There were tears in the girl's eyes. "Ma, you can't go alone. Carver's better'n thirty miles away!" She paused. "Look . . . iffen I can't talk you out of it, at least let me come with you."

The old woman sat silent for a while. Her face gave nothing away. The girl stood before her as the sun climbed higher, waiting expectantly.

"Climb aboard," her mother said at length.

They made slow, jolting progress toward Carver, the old woman grim and determined, the young girl helpless and afraid. That was why the old woman hadn't told her about the Henry repeater she'd hidden beneath the gunnysack under her seat. Because Bonnie was already frightened enough.

But when the time came, she'd know

her mother hadn't just come to Carver to tell the town about Hunter's past. She'd also come to use the rifle and kill the marshal for what he'd done to her poor, dead husband.

9

TOM came awake with a strange feeling in his belly; not an ache or a pain but a gut instinct he knew better than to ignore. He rose from the chair behind the desk, touching the butt of his new colt to make sure it was still there at his hip, and moved quickly across the office to look out into the street.

He could tell it was still early morning by the position of the shadows on the ground. At this hour the street was still deserted. Later, the town would busy-up with farmers, sheepmen and copper-miners in from neighbouring claims, and Carver would be all bustle. Now, however, the town lay silent and peaceful.

Willing himself to relax, Tom went out back to wash, but still couldn't shake the weird feeling. After he put coffee on to boil, he went back to his position at the window, feeling quiet and reflective.

Some strange and inexplicable sensation had told him that his business with Birchell would finally be settled today. One way or the other, his vengeance-quest would reach its climax.

And he was glad. Because all the waiting and near-constant vigilance was at last beginning to play on his nerves. It had started with Ed Judd's report in the *Star* about Ike Daggett's escape from jail. Judd had reported the events Beecher had told him all right, but he'd gone further, suggesting that Tom had driven Daggett to 'desperate lengths' by 'both verbal and physical intimidation' which had been witnessed by three 'understandably anonymous but nonetheless stalwart citizens' of town. He'd claimed that from the moment Tom had ridden into Carver, he'd been at loggerheads with Daggett, and that his use of his pistol was rapidly becoming 'a regular and unpleasant occurrence.'

Thankfully, the story hadn't had much effect. Sure, a couple of people had gone out of their way to ignore him, or crossed the street when they saw him coming along their side of the boardwalk but, for the most part, folks — who had no love for Daggett anyway — maintained their friendliness toward him. And the town council certainly had no complaints about how he was doing his job.

He had spoken to Denning twice in the past week, both times late at night, and in the deepest shadows on the outskirts of town. Although the federal lawman was now concentrating his attention on Birchell, however, he had nothing new to report. As far as he could tell, the freight boss was letting things run their course, and had apparently banished Tom from his mind.

But Birchell was up to something, Denning was sure. And whatever it was, he was keeping it deadly quiet.

Still, Tom had no patience for the waiting game he was being forced to play, and was anxious to make some progress towards clearing his name. He'd said as much to Denning.

"That's all well and good," the U.S. marshal had replied. "But sometimes the waiting game's the only one to play."

"There's got to be *some* way I can force Birchell's hand, though."

"I wouldn't advise it. You do something rash and Birchell's just canny enough to take advantage of it. Trust me. He'll make a mistake sooner or later. They always do."

"He hasn't made a mistake in the last six years," Tom replied bitterly.

"He made one," Denning pointed out. "He tried to frame you. I'd say that was his biggest mistake of all."

So they just continued to go about their business, the town marshal and the drifter in the leather vest, with no-one other than Clem Beecher aware that they were actually working together.

Fortunately, Zeb's good-humour had helped lighten Tom's load. Although the boy's position as his deputy was still unofficial, he was an invaluable aide. Sometime soon, the starpacker figured he would have to confess his past to *him*, too.

But all that was for the future. And right now, if his strange presentiment could be believed, Tom would soon find himself fully occupied with Birchell. Whichever way it turned out.

Meanwhile, Lee Knight was six miles outside town, and getting closer all the time.

Jason Birchell re-read the telegram with his lips pressed into a tight line, then screwed it up and threw it into the waste-basket. It was simple and straight to the point. *JOB OFFER ACCEPTED STOP EXPECT ME FOUR DAYS FROM THIS DATE.* It had been dated four days ago, but left unsigned.

The telegram meant a lot of things

to Birchell. It meant that Lee Knight would have taken care of Ike Daggett by now. It meant that before long he would be taking care of Tom Hunter, too. It meant that soon there'd be nobody left alive who could link him with the bullion job. It meant peace of mind.

At last.

All right; so maybe he'd been a fool. Maybe he should have just kept running and not gotten any fancy notions about setting someone up to take the blame for the stagecoach job. But when he'd seen that camp-fire set back from the main trail, the plan had just crept into his mind. The more he'd thought about it, the more he'd liked it. And when he saw the kid, it had seemed like the perfect set-up.

It had been well worth a bottle of whiskey to make things look good. He had half-buried the empty strong-box which he had left hidden in the shadows before riding up to the campsite — while the kid lay sleeping

228

off the booze. If he was lucky, it might throw whoever was pursuing him off his trail. At the very least, it would slow them down.

Only . . .

Abruptly he slammed a bunched fist against the wood of his desk. Only Hunter had been released from prison, come looking for him. And *found* him.

Still, there was no proof, nothing to link him with the bullion job. That was something, he guessed. But what if Hunter decided to take his advice, and settle things with his gun? There could be no more denying it, Birchell was scared. And he wouldn't stop being scared until Hunter was dead.

Almost without realising it, he had started to study his right hand. Six years, he thought. It had been a long time. A long time to go without using a gun. He'd slowed down a little, grown sloppy. But that wasn't why he'd hired Lee Knight. He'd hired Knight because he didn't want to involve himself in the coming fight. Complete detachment, that was it. Don't openly connect yourself with Hunter's death in any way at all.

He looked down at the waste-basket and then fished the ball of paper back out. Unfolding it, he re-read Knight's message again. Just seeing it there in print somehow bolstered his courage.

JOB OFFER ACCEPTED STOP EXPECT ME FOUR DAYS FROM THIS DATE.
Four days from this date.
Today.

Lee Knight was four miles outside town and approaching fast.

Travelling in a rickety old buckboard drawn by an ageing farm-horse beneath a burning sun and across a flat, unending wasteland had taken its toll of the old woman and her daughter. They sat hunched over in silence, their eyes narrowed against the glare of the sun on the bleached, lifeless land before them. That was pretty much how they had made the entire journey.

At night, they had cooked a small meal and ate in silence. Every time Bonnie tried to bring up the subject neither of them could stop thinking about, the old woman had refused to listen or reply. Her mind was made up. "Killin' must be in his blood," she would say. But she would say no more than that.

Now, as they started to roll down the slope into the shallow dip in which Carver had been built, the sight of civilisation gave them both renewed energy. The old woman's dark eyes lit up, and her daughter felt a brief sense of relief, which was soon overshadowed when she remembered the mission that had brought them here.

To ruin the man who'd killed her pa.

Glancing sideways, Bonnie experienced a new wave of disquiet. She had never seen her mother like this before, and it frightened her. Ma rarely if ever smiled. She never sang or stopped to admire the beauty of the desert. Ma just lived. It was as simple as that. She lived, and would continue living until the Good Lord decided otherwise.

When pa was here, things had been different, of course. But it had been so long since Bonnie had seen her mother filled with anticipation and purpose, that to see it now seemed somehow *unnatural*.

Slowly the buckboard trundled down onto level ground as they began their approach to Front Street. The sun had started its skyward climb and the town was coming to life. Folks crowded the sidewalks and kids hurried along to school. When they reached the first few buildings that marked the start of Front, the old woman tugged on the reins and the nag came to a halt. Pushing on the brake, she sat quietly and squinted along the street.

"Can't see 'im," she muttered.

Again Bonnie glanced at her grim

232

profile. She wanted to give voice to a lot of the things that had built up inside her during the past few days, but she knew that whatever she said wouldn't change matters one bit. So she remained silent, willing, albeit reluctantly, to follow her mother's lead.

A man who had been lounging on the porch opposite looked over at them, watching them with frank interest. Bonnie was about to look away from him when he stepped down into the street and walked over to them. He looked to be about thirty or so; dark, good-looking and dressed cowhand fashion.

He touched the brim of his hat. "Morning, ladies."

The old woman just stared at him.

"Excuse me, ma am," he said, "but would your name be McGiff?"

"Do I know you?" the old woman replied warily.

"No, ma'am. But I'd appreciate a few words." Quickly, before she could refuse, he brought out a wallet, slipped it open and waited just long enough for her to see the shield it contained before putting it away again. "My name is Philip Denning, ma'am. I'm a United States marshal. I don't know what's brought you to town, but I'm glad I've seen you, because it gives me the chance to set the record straight with you about someone."

Now the old woman's eyes were suspicious slits. "Who?"

"Tom Hunter," Denning told her.

Two miles outside town, Lee Knight reined in and paused just long enough to wet his lips with the last of the water in his canteen. He figured to hit Carver within the half-hour.

The law office door burst open at nine thirty-five.

The man who came hustling in looked red-faced and sweaty. His name was Benteen and he worked at the *Star*, setting type and working the small press. He was of medium height and stocky build, with thinning brown hair and a wide, smiling face.

Except that he wasn't smiling at the moment.

"Morning, Mr Benteen," Tom nodded cautiously. "What's the trouble?"

Benteen was breathing hard. "A message, marshal," he gasped. "F . . . for you. From . . . from a man across the street in our o — office."

Tom came up out of his Douglas chair fast, the circulars mailed to him by the county sheriff left forgotten on his desk. "Spit it out, then," he said tersely.

Benteen jerked a thumb over his shoulder. "In the office," he repeated. "A man. Came in about five minutes ago." Flustered, he shook his head to clear it. "Cool as ice, he was. Just sashayed in and told me to set up a headline for the next edition of the paper." He was sweating so bad that he had to stop to wipe his leaking face. "Told me to set up a headline that said, 'Town Marshal Dies In Gunfight'."

Tom frowned. "This . . . this feller got a name?"

"Knight," Benteen said, anxious to get everything out. "Lee Knight. He told me to tell you to ask someone who Lee Knight was, 'cause you probably wouldn't know on account of . . . " he faltered.

"Go on," Tom demanded.

With visible discomfort, Benteen said, "He said you probably wouldn't know him on account of you havin' spent the last six years in prison."

"*What?*" asked Zeb, slack-jawed. He had just finished sweeping out the cell-block. Now he stood in the doorway, gripping the broom tightly. "Whoever he is, this Knight must be loco — "

"He ain't loco," Tom said flatly. He could feel Zeb's clear blue eyes on him, but ignored the boy. There was no time for explanations now.

"*Do* you know Knight?" asked Benteen.

"Know *of* him," Tom confessed. "He's a gunfighter. Been around the

Territory for I don't know how long. I've heard that he kills for pleasure as much as anything else. And he always challenges his targets to a face-to-face showdown. Never any back-shooting."

"Targets?" asked Zeb.

"Uh-huh. He's a killer-for-hire, Zeb. Kind of like a bounty-hunter."

"Is he wanted?"

"I doubt it. He's too clever for that, if all's to be believed. Oh, he kills, sure. But always in self-defence. Like I said, he always gives his targets a chance to fight back."

Benteen threw a nervous glance over his shoulder, back the way he'd come. "He's fast, is he?"

"Greased lightning — so they say," Tom replied. "Was that all he told you to tell me?"

Benteen shook his head. "He said he'll be out on Front at ten o'clock, waiting for you."

"All right, Benteen. Thanks for running the message. You can go now. And tell Knight I'll be out there at ten sharp."

Benteen paused. "Marshal?" he asked quietly. Tom knew what was coming. "Marshal, is it true what Knight said? 'Bout prison, I mean?"

"It's true," Tom said after a pause. "But there's more to it than that." He eyed the clock on the wall. "Maybe I'll tell you and, your editor all about it thirty minutes from now."

When Benteen had gone, Tom went to the window and looked out. Up the street he could see a man in denims lounging in the doorway of the newspaper office. Lee Knight, eh? Now he understood why Birchell had been so damn' quiet lately. He'd hired a killer to settle matters for him in a gunfight.

Softly, Tom said, "Zeb, go get Clem Beecher. Tell him what Benteen just told us, and tell him to find Denning and get back here as quick as they can."

But Zeb remained locked where he

was. "*Prison*, Tom?" he asked. The disappointment in his voice was like a knife in Tom's guts. "And who . . . who's Denning?"

"Beecher'll explain everything," Tom said, checking the time again. It was nine forty-two. "Now *hurry*, Zeb. I've got to go out there twenty minutes from now, and I want to make sure Beecher and Denning know what's going on."

When the boy left, Tom paced the office slowly. He had the feeling that this was going to be the longest twenty minutes of his life. And if Knight was as good as they said, it might also be his last.

It was obvious from Beecher's tight-lipped expression that Zeb had told him exactly what had happened. The mayor looked angry and just a little scared as he came into the office ten minutes later with Zeb at his heels.

Mirrored in the young deputy's face were all the emotions Beecher was experiencing. It was all out in the open now; the youngster knew that this was about more than just another gunfighter looking to make trouble.

"Where's Denning?" Tom demanded.

"Couldn't find him," Beecher replied. He indicated the wall-clock. "Not in the amount of time we've got left."

"All right. It doesn't matter."

The room grew silent as the starpacker took his Colt from its holster and checked it over one last time. He should have guessed it would all end with a gun. Guns had played such a big part in it already; why shouldn't they have the last word?

Beecher watched him through troubled eyes. Then he said to Zeb, "Break out two of them long guns, boy."

"Sure, Mr Beecher." The fair-haired youngster headed for the rifle-rack until Tom called his name and stopped him to his tracks.

"Leave it, Zeb. I don't want either of you two getting involved."

"But — "

"*Leave* it, I said. This is between me and Knight. And after that, me and Birchell."

The mayor eyed the floorboards. "Do you, ah . . . do you think you're fast enough, Tom?"

The clock began to strike ten.

"Let's just wait and see, shall we?" Tom replied grimly.

All three of them exchanged heavy, expressive glances. Then, without another word, Tom pulled on his hat and went across to the door.

"Tom?" It was Zeb.

The lawman looked back.

"Good luck," said the youngster.

Tom nodded, opened the door and stepped outside.

Word must have spread, because the street was deserted. A faint breeze, sending the dust skittering along Front, provided the only movement. Tom licked his lips, adjusting his gunbelt slightly until it felt not so much comfortable, as *right*. Then he stepped

241

forward, slowly, his boots making hollow, empty sounds on the boardwalk.

That's when he saw Knight about eighty feet up on the other side of the street. The gunman was almost a mirror-image of himself, coming out from beneath the porch overhang to step down into the street and walk unhurriedly to its deserted centre. When Knight reached the midway point, he stood with legs spread slightly, thumbs tucked into his weapons belt, head to one side, insolent and challenging.

Tom's grey-blue eyes flicked briefly to left and right. He saw faces watching him through dusty windows, and wondered exactly what they'd heard and what they were thinking. Whose side were they on? Did they feel frightened or excited? Did it matter to them if he survived or died in the dust?

He looked over at Birchell's office and saw the fat man waiting anxiously at his window. Birchell's face looked strained and anxious. He didn't consider the outcome of this fight a foregone conclusion, then. There was still an element of doubt. Tom turned his attention back to Knight, wondering where in hell Denning had gotten to, and then he stepped out into the sunlight and came to a halt twenty yards from the gunman.

"I don't want to fight you," he said calmly.

"Don't, then," Knight replied, his long, thin face splitting in a grin. "Just you stand where you are and let me do all the work."

"I've got no quarrel with you."

Knight gave a small, one-shouldered shrug. "What's that got to do with it?"

There was no avoiding this, then.

Tom shifted his attention from Knight's bearded face to his legs. It was the mistake so many gunfighters made, spending their time watching their opponents eyes. It was their legs that gave them away. The minute they shifted balance, you knew they were going to reach for their guns. That was your cue to slap leather and kill them first.

Instinctively he went into a crouch, his arms held away from his body for balance. His right hand formed a claw above his Colt. He licked his lips.

This was it, then; the moment when you turned sideways-on to present a smaller target; the moment you drew your gun and used it not to shoot the tops off Apache plumes or shatter empty bottles but, quite simply, to kill.

There was a movement off to his right. He didn't want to take his eyes off Knight, but he had to know who was there. He glanced over to find out, beads of sweat shining on his serious face as the climbing sun beat down on them harshly.

There, on the boardwalk, stood Denning, not fully understanding what was going on. Next to him stood a young girl who seemed vaguely familiar. And next to her . . .

All at once Tom went cold; so cold that it felt as if he'd been buried up to his neck in snow.

It was the old woman with the jet-black eyes.

That was when Knight drew his right-side .38 with staggering speed and fired his first shot of the contest.

The young girl screamed, but incredibly, the bullet missed. Tom lurched to one side, to throw Knight's aim off still further. This time, however, the gunman had found his range, and as gun-thunder filled their ears again, Tom gave a grunt of pain and stumbled backwards.

Warm blood spilled down his right side. He became aware of it only as he crumpled earthward with his face screwed into a mask of agony.

He heard Knight re-cocking his gun for the killing shot, but with teeth clenched against the pain, too stubborn to give in to it, he finally drew his own weapon, brought it up and squeezed the trigger.

Knight's eyes opened wide and Tom saw surprise and fear crowded into them. As his gunblast tore the muggy morning air apart, Tom got back onto his feet and fired twice more.

The bullets *thwacked* into Knight's narrow chest. He left the ground and flew back a couple of feet, his gun falling to the ground. The exit holes in his back were large and messy; they clogged with sand when he fell, dead, to the ground.

Tom swayed slightly, then turned to look briefly at Denning. The federal lawman stood frozen in the act of drawing his .44. Their eyes met, but they said nothing. Denning slipped his gun back into leather. There was no need for it now. But before he could go to the starpacker's aid, Tom wheeled drunkenly, feeling the wetness of his blood staining his shirt and pants'-leg, and started towards Birchell's office.

As Lee Knight hit the dirt, Birchell's groan came out, full of despair.

Knight had been his last hope. Knight had been the best. Knight —

Knight was *dead*.

And Hunter had started moving Birchell's way, the wound in his side apparently not slowing him down at all. Even at this distance Birchell could see the fury in his eyes.

Sweat trickled sluggishly down the freight boss's face. He had almost convinced himself that Hunter's showdown with Knight would be the climax of the whole affair, but he'd been wrong. Hunter's confrontation with Birchell *himself* would end it all.

It was going to be Hunter against the hunted.

As he fought to control the trembling of his hands, he told himself that he might still be able to bluff his way out of it. He fumbled in his jacket pocket and brought out his Colt. With the gun held behind his back, he moved out of the office and onto the boardwalk. He saw white faces peering curiously at him from windows and doorways but thrust them from his mind.

His voice was quite steady when he said, "You all right, marshal?"

The sound of his voice made Tom halt sharply. Some of the fury in his eyes died. He swayed slightly as he stood there, the Frontier Colt still clasped firmly in his hand.

There were two bullets in that gun, he thought. And as far as he was concerned, Birchell was going to get them both. Justice wouldn't beat Birchell. He saw that now. The fat man had covered his tracks too well, so that no evidence was left to point the accusing finger. Birchell's only justice would be a bullet. He started to lift the gun.

Then he heard footsteps behind him and glanced sideways as Denning trotted up beside him. Something was shining on Denning's vest. It was his badge. Tom turned his attention back to Birchell, whose eyes had gone wide in surprise. The fat man's mouth was shaped like a downward-curving horseshoe.

"All right, Birchell. You can't bluff your way out of it this time. We've got all the evidence we need." Denning's voice was deep and authoritative.

Tom blinked, his mind woozy with loss of blood. Evidence? *What* evidence? What the hell was Denning talking about?

Then he had it — he thought. Denning was warning Birchell against trying a bluff, when all the time *he* was making the biggest bluff of all, to force Birchell into a corner!

"Evidence?" Birchell faltered. "There . . . there must be some misunderstanding . . . "

He hadn't reckoned on a U.S. marshal turning up. He might have been able to rely on his freighters to help him before, but he knew they wouldn't lift a linger against a federal lawman. He was on his own. Again he said, "Evidence? I don't under — "

"You'll understand it all soon

enough," Denning bluffed. He was deadly serious. "But it means I can arrest you for two killings and a robbery. The same crimes you set the marshal here up for six years ago.

"*No!*"

"Yes," Denning said coldly. He smiled.

"What the hell evidence have you got, then?" Birchell asked. "There isn't any! Why, I . . . I don't even know what you're talking about. It's all a pack of lies!"

"We'll see about that — in court." Denning took a step forward and Birchell stiffened.

"You're bluffing! You're trying to set *me* up!" Inside, the freight boss was ice-cold, trying frantically to remember exactly what he'd said in his wire to Knight. Maybe *that* was the evidence they were talking about. But it *couldn't* be! There was nothing in that telegram that — "You're bluffing," he said again. "You haven't got any evidence. I was too damn' careful for that!"

He bit off abruptly, dumbstruck. But it was too late. He'd said it now — yelled it, more like. And very slowly he became aware that folks had come outside again, onto the street, and were standing on the boardwalks, watching him. If they didn't have any idea what was going on before, they were piecing it all together now.

He turned to face them one by one; Beecher, Zeb Coulson, Della Vine, Judd, Hobart, Greaves, Faulkner, Keegan, Casey and all the rest, and knew he'd said more than enough. He'd been betrayed by his own big mouth.

"*All right!*" he yelled abruptly. "All right, figure it out! But remember this . . . " His voice cracked a little. "Remember that I got away with it . . . for six years . . . "

Then the gun was out in front of him and he was aiming it at Tom and Denning. "You clever bastards," he muttered. "You think you're so clever, I bet!" He nodded and gave a

251

crazy laugh. "See where your cleverness has got you now?" He pulled the trigger and the gun roared.

Denning fell away like a dead leaf in an autumn wind. He hit the dust and rolled hard. Everyone behind Tom stood frozen with shock, unable to do anything except watch.

Just as Tom lifted his Colt, Birchell fired again, and he felt himself punched savagely in the right shoulder and sent in a giddy half-circle. There was a burning flame in his right arm. He couldn't move it. He brought his left hand across, trying to wrestle the gun from the useless grip of his right, but even as he looked up at Birchell, the freight boss aimed his .45 for the kill.

Tom cursed silently. He just couldn't break his own grip on the Colt to get it into his left hand. Denning, behind him, was trying to roll onto his back and fumble his .44 from leather but it was no good, he wouldn't be fast enough.

Birchell wore a mad grin as he

thumbed back the hammer —

Before he could fire, however, a bullet pushed him backwards into the wall of his office.

The gun fell from his hand as he clutched at the red stain on his chest. He took a couple of unsteady steps along the boardwalk and then the unseen gun boomed again and Tom saw his chest explode, almost dead centre. The fat man looked stunned, then scared. A moment later he collapsed in a red heap and lay still.

There was no sound, no movement, just the smell of death in the air. Tom craned his neck slowly, expecting to find Beecher standing there, or maybe even Zeb, a gun still smoking in his hand.

He didn't expect to see the old woman with the piercing black eyes.

Smoke drifted from her Henry repeater like a ghostly serpent. Slowly, she lowered the rifle until she held it across her ample belly, and when she walked towards him he tried to read an expression or an emotion on her lined face, but couldn't.

He struggled to his feet as she came up and stood staring into his face. He was pale and weak and there were two bullets in him that would have to be dug out. God alone knew how Denning was, but at least he was moving and swearing, and that was good.

"Seems like what that lawman told me 'bout you was right," the old woman allowed. "'Pears I was blamin' you fer somethin' you never had nothin' to do with." She gave a shrug. "'M sorry," she said with a nod. Then she turned her eyes toward Birchell's corpse, but there was no horror or revulsion in her as she looked down at him. "I come to town to kill the man who kilt my husband," she muttered to no-one in particular. "Reckon I did it."

Then, before she turned away, he looked into her eyes, and although they were still as black as ever, they no longer reminded him of pits leading to hell. She and her shocked daughter disappeared into the sudden surge of townsfolk rushing to his aid.

He was forgiven, proven innocent, and among friends. But most of all he was *tired*. He looked down at Denning, who was trying to staunch the flow of blood coming from a hole in the top of his left leg, and asked, "How are you feeling?"

"Lousy," Denning complained sourly. But then, very suddenly, he summoned a grin. "How about you?"

Tom glanced down at the crimson stains on his shirt and pants. His side had gone numb but there was still a burning ache in his shoulder. He felt battered, bruised and tired. But, after studying the federal lawman a moment, he said. "I never felt better," and they both smiled, because they knew that what he said was the absolute truth.

FIGHTING RAMROD
Charles N. Heckelmann

Most men would have cut their losses, but Frazer counted the bullets in his guns and said he'd soak the range in blood before he'd give up another inch of what was his.

LONE GUN
Eric Allen

Smoke Blackbird had been away too long. The Lequires had seized the Blackbird farm, forcing the Indians and settlers off, and no one seemed willing to fight! He had to fight alone.

THE THIRD RIDER
Barry Cord

Mel Rawlins wasn't going to let anything stand in his way. His father was murdered, his two brothers gone. Now Mel rode for vengeance.

ARIZONA DRIFTERS
W. C. Tuttle

When drifting Dutton and Lonnie Steelman decide to become partners they find that they have a common enemy in the formidable Thurston brothers.

TOMBSTONE
Matt Braun

Wells Fargo paid Luke Starbuck to outgun the silver-thieving stagecoach gang at Tombstone. Before long Luke can see the only thing bearing fruit in this eldorado will be the gallows tree.

HIGH BORDER RIDERS
Lee Floren

Buckshot McKee and Tortilla Joe cut the trail of a border tough who was running Mexican beef into Texas. They stopped the smuggler in his tracks.

BRETT RANDALL, GAMBLER
E. B. Mann

Larry Day had the choice of running away from the law or of assuming a dead man's place. No matter what he decided he was bound to end up dead.

THE GUNSHARP
William R. Cox

The Eggerleys weren't very smart. They trained their sights on Will Carney and Arizona's biggest blood bath began.

THE DEPUTY OF SAN RIANO
Lawrence A. Keating and
Al. P. Nelson

When a man fell dead from his horse, Ed Grant was spotted riding away from the scene. The deputy sheriff rode out after him and came up against everything from gunfire to dynamite.

FARGO: MASSACRE RIVER
John Benteen

The ambushers up ahead had now blocked the road. Fargo's convoy was a jumble, a perfect target for the insurgents' weapons!

SUNDANCE: DEATH IN THE LAVA
John Benteen

The Modoc's captured the wagon train and its cargo of gold. But now the halfbreed they called Sundance was going after it . . .

HARSH RECKONING
Phil Ketchum

Five years of keeping himself alive in a brutal prison had made Brand tough and careless about who he gunned down . . .

FARGO: PANAMA GOLD
John Benteen

With foreign money behind him, Buckner was going to destroy the Panama Canal before it could be completed. Fargo's job was to stop Buckner.

FARGO:
THE SHARPSHOOTERS
John Benteen

The Canfield clan, thirty strong were raising hell in Texas. Fargo was tough enough to hold his own against the whole clan.

PISTOL LAW
Paul Evan Lehman

Lance Jones came back to Mustang for just one thing — revenge! Revenge on the people who had him thrown in jail.

HELL RIDERS
Steve Mensing

Wade Walker's kid brother, Duane, was locked up in the Silver City jail facing a rope at dawn. Wade was a ruthless outlaw, but he was smart, and he had vowed to have his brother out of jail before morning!

DESERT OF THE DAMNED
Nelson Nye

The law was after him for the murder of a marshal — a murder he didn't commit. Breen was after him for revenge — and Breen wouldn't stop at anything . . . blackmail, a frameup . . . or murder.

DAY OF THE COMANCHEROS
Steven C. Lawrence

Their very name struck terror into men's hearts — the Comancheros, a savage army of cutthroats who swept across Texas, leaving behind a bloodstained trail of robbery and murder.

SUNDANCE: SILENT ENEMY
John Benteen

A lone crazed Cheyenne was on a personal war path. They needed to pit one man against one crazed Indian. That man was Sundance.

LASSITER
Jack Slade

Lassiter wasn't the kind of man to listen to reason. Cross him once and he'll hold a grudge for years to come — if he let you live that long.

LAST STAGE TO GOMORRAH
Barry Cord

Jeff Carter, tough ex-riverboat gambler, now had himself a horse ranch that kept him free from gunfights and card games. Until Sturvesant of Wells Fargo showed up.

McALLISTER ON THE COMANCHE CROSSING
Matt Chisholm

The Comanche, McAllister owes them a life — and the trail is soaked with the blood of the men who had tried to outrun them before.

QUICK-TRIGGER COUNTRY
Clem Colt

Turkey Red hooked up with Curly Bill Graham's outlaw crew. But wholesale murder was out of Turk's line, so when range war flared he bucked the whole border gang alone . . .

CAMPAIGNING
Jim Miller

Ambushed on the Santa Fe trail, Sean Callahan is saved by two Indian strangers. But there'll be more lead and arrows flying before the band join Kit Carson against the Comanches.